This is a work of fiction. The ch...
invented.

Facebook fan page /Theresa"Reese"Kirk
Email: reese326@yahoo.com
Twitter: @Reese_326
Cover design: Cloudsurferz Media
Self-publishing Author
Website: https://squareup.com/store/TheresaReese

Acknowledgements:

I want to give a Shout out to my readers who continue to support me... I wouldn't be who I am without your feedback and criticism. My cuzzo Shawna who nearly killed me to release The Refill (lol), my cuzzo Felicia whose my twin and the other entrepreneur in the fam., my girl Cory, my babies Hazel and Anna (10+ years of friendship). My coworkers Shakia, Dawn, Shameeka, Tammy, Chanda, Rhonda, Glenda, Pat, Tila and Jackie for the encouragement plus many more... My newly published authors Clarice and Naisha, my bmore sisters Chantelle and Danielle. My Patterson people it's way too many to name and I can't forget that's my home. Family is always #1 in my eyes. Special thanks to Let's Talk Reality crew for having me on air Kat, Unique and Mo. Kat thanks for the many brief talks.

My crew BWSN (Kisha, Alison, Christina, Simone and Carla) plus 1 Adia all different yet so similar, I love you ladies :)...

Last but not least my Binky butt because she is on my back about not being able to read my books... Mommy will write one just for you!!! Let's take it to the top

Previously...

"So who's the father?"...
"I'm blaming that on that 1 glass of wine and 2 shots of Patron".

And that's exactly how my naive ass ended up in this predicament...

"Girl, I don't know. I slept with both of them the same night, unprotected, but I've been sexing Khalil the most, so I hope it's his"
"Pilar you could have gotten a disease. Fuck being pregnant!" Lola chastised.
"Lola, I know and I'm already embarrassed and disappointed in myself, but Khalil saw the test in the bathroom garbage!" I thought about how careless I had been.
"Well, what does it add up to?"
"I'm 13 weeks, so hopefully, I was already pregnant when I had sex with Avery, but that just makes me feel dirtier."
"What do you mean 'hopefully'? I hope you plan on getting a DNA test, Pilar?"
"Lola I'm not putting my baby through that and if Kha found out I tested the baby, he would fuck me up!" I whined.

"That's the least of your worries, if that baby happens to come out looking just like Avery." Lola shook her head in disbelief.

"Listen I know I was careless but what can I do now? I can't get rid of it. He knows."

"Tell him that you will not bring a baby into a situation that's already fucked up. Get rid of it and there you are all set" Lola pointed her finger in my face.

"Right, but you started this Lola!" Pilar yelled, in frustration.

Pointing her finger at herself, Lola asked: "Me, now how the fuck do you blame this on me Pilar? I said date, not fuck on the first night!" Lola yelled, grabbing up her belongings.

I grabbed Lola's hand, so that she wouldn't walk out of the room. "Lola, please, stay! I'm sorry. I'm scared and I feel alone. You're the only one who knows what's going on, besides my girl Jewel, who won't be here for another month. So, please, don't leave me, Lola." I pleaded, hoping she would change her mind.

"Listen, chick, I don't think your irrational ass needs to be having anybody's baby, right now. Get it together P, before you get caught up in some shit."

"Yeah, I know but I'm going to keep it. I'll just deal with the consequences, later."

I plopped down on the bed, looking at the paper in my hands...

A year later

Giving birth was exactly what I needed to get my life back on track. Rue Monroe Taylor entered this world on June 23rd, kicking and screaming.

-Now why would I give her Khalil's last name when I didn't know who the father was? Well, truth be told, I had no choice because he's my husband. Thank God, when she came-out, she looked just like Khalil, down to the freckles on her cheeks.

"Thank God!" I silently mouthed, as I held her in my arms, looking down at her, thinking I had beaten the game.

"Can I hold my daughter, Pilar? You carried her for 9 months, damn!" Khalil scrunched up his nose at me, holding out his arms.

"Fine Khalil, you forgot to mention I did all the damn work, too!" I stated, matter of factly, handing Rue to him.

Watching the way he cradled her made my heart melt. I don't know what would have happened, had she not been his.

The next few months went by, smoothly. I stayed under the radar and raised my kids.

Ring! Ring!

"Hello!" I yelled into the phone, over the running water.

"Hey, hunny! I'll be flying in this weekend, so I hope you're ready to show me a good time!!"

"Yes, girl, I can't wait!" I geeked, blushing.

"I can't believe it's been 10 years since I've seen you!"

"Well, you better get ready because I'm coming to turn all the way up!" Jewel yelled.

I chuckled. "I know, girl, it will be the first time I'm going out after giving birth and I can use this excitement!"

"Yes, boo. Well, let me let you get back to motherhood. I'll be in touch." Jewel ended the call.

The partying, drinking and vibing is just what I need. I have been cooped-up in the house with my family so long that I couldn't stay up pass 10pm. Don't get me wrong, it has been great. Khalil has changed and we've actually gotten pass all of the drama. Liam is quite the helper with Rue and Andre hasn't bothered me, since I blocked his number. My email snapped me out of my trance, alerting me that I had an unread message.

- Hello, beautiful! I don't know what it was that abruptly ended things, but I want to see you again. You have avoided me for way to long.

-Ave

"Shit, he just won't stop." I hissed, rolling my eyes. Yes, I'm guilty of avoiding Avery. Hell, I was scared he would tell Kha about our one night stand. Just like all the unanswered messages, I wouldn't reply to this one either.

"That's some dirt I'd like to stay buried." I muttered. As I closed my laptop, I heard the front door slam shut, causing me to jump.

"Nah, fuck that. He can get handled too!" Khalil yelled out in frustration.

"Say no more my nigga, if that's what you want to do, that's what we gon do!" Tony replied.

"Yeah, I'm on it, but keep it down. The less wifey knows, the better." Don assured them.

Listening-in from the kitchen, I knew some shit was about to pop-off, but I didn't know with who.

"Her ass gon' find-out, 'cause Dre done crossed the line, stepping his feet on my grounds, knowing that's where I do my work. I tried to be nice, but he gon' learn. I'm not to be fucked with!" Khalil boasted.

Cupping my mouth, I was shocked to hear Khalil bring up Dre. I haven't heard from him in damn near a year. Word on the street was he got locked up again, but apparently that wasn't true.

"Listen Kha, you not supposed to get your hands dir-"
Khalil cut Tony off, before he could finish.
"Fuck that! This is personal. If I gotta put the bullet in his head myself, I'm going to handle him!"
"Nah, Kha! You don't have to do all that. I told you, I'll handle it!" Tony motioned his hands at himself.
"We gon' discuss this, but at a later date. Let me go see how wifey and the kids are." Khalil got up and headed to the door, letting them out.
"A'ight holla at me!" They dapped fists.
"One!"

Watching to make sure the guys were gone, I came out into the living room.
"Hey baby, how was your day?" I tipped-toed to kiss Kha.
"Stressed, P. But that's here nor there." Khalil let out a sigh as he flopped down on the

couch. Straddling him, I lifted his chin, so he could look in my eyes.

"Baby, what's bothering you? Talk to me. Don't shut me out, Kha." I insisted, although I already knew pretty much of what was going on.

"Nothing that I want to stress you about ma-ma, but, since you feel like being nice, straddling a brother, are you going to come and take care of me?" Khalil joked, palming my butt.

I hopped-up off of him, playfully slapping him. "Boy, please, do you know it's almost time for Rue's feeding?"

"Yeah you go feed her and then come feed daddy, cuz I'm hungry for this." Khalil groped at my box.

"Kha, quit. I will give you some attention, after I feed my baby." Heading towards the stairs, I glanced back in Khalil's direction. "Baby, are you sure you're ok?"

"Yes girl I'm sure. Trust me, I'm good, Ma!" Khalil reassured me.

"Promise?"

"I promise, Pilar." Khalil sighed.

Knowing Khalil was lying was eating away at me. I hated the fact that he just couldn't let this beef go with Andre. I mean in the end, Khalil won. I was his woman, Khalil was raising our son and I had just given birth to our daughter. That just wasn't enough. No, it just wasn't. He let his pride and ego get in the way.

"Men." I thought, as I entered Rue's nursery and saw her lying there playing with her mobile.

"Hi, mommy's baby. You're up all by yourself, being such a good baby!" I lifted her up, as I made my way to the rocking chair. Listening to her coo, got me all warm inside.

"So, I take it you're not hungry, huh? You just talking all day long." I said to Rue, while laying her in my lap. That's when she started fussing, causing me to laugh.

"Spoiled butt, don't even wanna lay down!" I grabbed her bottle out of the warmer and fed her, until she fell back asleep. Just then, Khalil entered the room.

"Is she out?" Khalil grabbed Rue out of my arms, rocking her from side to side.

"Baby, I'm going to shower. You can change her and lay her down. She's all set." I said, looking at him, as he rocked her. "Okay, baby girl! Do your thang!" I don't know how he does it. He was on a rampage and now, here he was, being gentle with our baby.

"Baby, wake-up." I felt a tap on my shoulder. I jumped, not realizing I had fallen asleep in the bath tub.

"Huh? Uhh, okay, I'm up." Stretching out my arms, I hopped-up. The temperature of the water caught me off guard.

"I didn't even know I had fell asleep, babe." I stated, wrapping the towel around my body.

"I can tell, Pilar." I watched Khalil wash his face and head to the room. I was on his heels.

"What's wrong with you, Kha? Why are you giving me attitude?" I walked up on Khalil, tapping his shoulder.

"This is the 3rd night in a row, Pilar." He signaled with 3 fingers, as he put emphasis on 'the third'.

"Okay, Khalil, I was tired." I closed the door behind me, trying not to make too much noise and wake the kids.

"Your ass is always tired, feeding the baby, cooking or playing with Liam. But here it is a nigga can't get no attention from his lady." Khalil said nonchalantly.

Jumping in front of Khalil, I tried to hold on to the towel and poke him, as I spoke. "Really Kha? I just gave birth to our daughter 3 months ago and you iggin me about some pussy? Like, you can't be serious, right now!" I stood face to face with Khalil.

"Get your little ass out of my face, Pilar. I'm not in the mood for your silly ass!" nudging me to the side. I lost my balance and fell on the bed.

"Oh, so that's how you doing things, Kha? You can get your shit and get out, if you feeling like that!" picking up the remote off of the bed and tossing it at Khalil. It hit him in his chest.

"Pilar, I done told your ass about hitting me with things. I'ma knock you out, you keep it up!" Placing the remote on the dresser, Khalil turned his back to me. I taunted him a little more.

"Just like how you going to knock-out Andre when you see him, huh?" I shouted. Turning around, he ran up on me, pinning me down on the bed.

"Say that shit again, Pilar and I'm going to fuck you up! You don't know shit so don't say shit. If I hear you've been around him I will kill you, Pilar!" I tried to fight Khalil off of me, to no avail.

"Do you hear me? Do you?" Khalil pressed down on my wrists, as he had his knees on my legs.

"Pilar I'm not going to repeat myself, stay the fuck out of it!"

"Get off of me, Khalil!" I moved my arms, trying to break free. He let-up on me. I got up and grabbed the towel and my night shirt and headed out of the bedroom.

"Get back in here, Pilar!" Khalil shouted, after me.

I ignored him and went into the bathroom downstairs, shutting the door behind me. Massaging my wrist, I let the tears fall.

I can't believe he had just blacked-out, all because I haven't been giving him any. Sighing, I glanced at the mirror, inwardly questioning if staying with Khalil was worth it...

I got up extra early to get the kids ready to go to my mother's house before 8am. I needed my first day back at work to go smoothly. I moved swiftly and quietly, so that I wouldn't wake Khalil. I was trying to avoid facing him this morning.

"Mommy, can I say bye to daddy?" Liam asked, grabbing up his bag, heading towards the staircase.

"No." I said, pulling him back, motioning my finger over my lips to silence Liam. "C'mon, daddy had a long night, you will see him later."

Slouching his shoulders, Liam was sad, but I knew I didn't want to see Khalil right now. "Okay, Mom."

I was in deep thought, driving to my mother's house. I let out a sigh, as I pulled up to the house. "Hey, Mom, thanks for being up this early." I gave her a little smile.

"Now, who else was going to keep these kids?" My mother joked.

"I know, right?" I handed my mom the car seat and the baby bag. I gave Liam a peck on the forehead.

I was back on the road. Maternity leave was up and honestly, I missed work. Being up under Khalil for the last few months had its up and downs. Khalil had become so moody and overprotective. I was just ready for a little peace of mind, but my luck had other plans.

"Hey girl, welcome back!" Marie squealed, in her squeaky voice. Any other time, I'd be annoyed at her being so chipper, but today I welcomed it.

"Hey, Mama!" I reached out to hug her. "So what's new?" I questioned, removing my purse from my shoulder and sitting it on my desk.

"Girl same ol' shit, different day, but..." She was cut-off by another voice.

"It's hard tracking you down, Pilar!" a sarcastic voice replied.

I turned around swiftly and was smack, dab in front of him.

"Uhh Aver- Avery, what are you doing here?" I stumbled over my words, caught by surprise.

"I've been looking for you, Pilar." Giving me the once over, Avery licked his lips as I felt uneasy.

Marie pulled me in whispering, "I was about to warn you girl!"

"So, wassup? What can I do for you, Avery?" Clasping my hands together, giving him a half smile.

"Can I talk to you for a minute, Pilar?" Avery stepped aside, as I made my way from behind the desk, leading him to a quiet space where we could talk. Everyone we passed was happy for my return.

"Hey, honey, how's the new baby girl? I know you miss her already!" a coworker said. All I could do was smile and nod.

Standing outside of the clinic, I faced Avery. "What did you want to talk about? What we did shouldn't have happened, Avery, I'm sorry." I said all in one breath, hoping he would leave me alone.

"Damn, it's like that? I thought we had something, baby-face, then out of the blue you stop taking my calls and I can't see you anymore." Avery said, out of frustration.

"Okay, relax, Avery. I stopped because I got back with my man. It's that simple." I said nonchalantly.

"So, fuck me, huh? Does he know you fucked me, Pilar? Does he?" Avery paced back and forth.

"Why the hell would he know that? We weren't together, so it was not for him to know. What the fuck is your problem? You here acting like a bitch, Avery." I turned to walk away, fed up.

Avery grabbed my arm. "Baby-face, listen, I came off wrong but damn, you had a nigga thinking otherwise!"

Yanking my arm from his grasp, "Nigga, you don't know me to be grabbing me like that! I said it's over, so leave it alone!" I was beyond pissed that he had brought me out of character, at my work place.

"Forget it? Forget it? Nah, baby girl, that coochie was too good to forget!" He laughed to himself, swaying from side to side.

"Avery, leave me alone!" I said, sucking my teeth and walking off.

"I fucked a looney bin." I mumbled, shaking my head.

Avery ran-up behind me, shouting. "Baby-face!"

I stopped at the security guard, letting them know I was being harassed, as I pointed at Avery walking in my direction.

"Sir, I'm going to have to ask you to leave the premises." the guard stated, stepping in front of him.

"Nah, my man, I'm talking to my girl." Avery swatted the guard's hand away, shouting after me, "Baby-face! It's like that? Cool, I'ma come see you real soon!"

Rolling my eyes, I flopped down in my chair, thinking "What the fuck did I get myself into?"

Slipping into a daydream, I was snapped out of my trance by Kha's voice.

"Pilar, hello. Why the hell you leave this morning without saying goodbye?"

I jumped-up, checking frantically, to see if Avery was anywhere in sight.

"I wasn't in the mood Kha. I had enough from you last night." I huffed, as I went to grab a few of the patient charts.

Khalil followed behind me, as I called a few patients, then whispered in my ear, "Baby, I don't want to argue or fight. How can I fix this?" Khalil pulled me close.

"You can't." I stated matter-of-factly.

"C'mon P. Don't do me like that. I miss my wife." Khalil said, sincerely.

"You miss me so much that you bruised my wrist, huh? All you can do to get back on my good side is to allow me to enjoy my weekend with my girl, Jewel."

Leaning over the counter, Khalil posted up beside me. "Aight, bet! Say no more, little mama. Can I get a kiss? I'ma check you when you come home." Khalil puckered his lips as I gave him a peck.

"Okay then, later!"

As Khalil walked away, I was relived that he hadn't run into Avery, nor did he put up a fight about me not feeling him.

"Girl, what the hell happened?" Marie slapped my arm, playfully.

"Hell if I know!" I chuckled, shaking my head at Marie.

- Damn I have too much damn drama in my life. I gave a looney bin some coochie, now he won't leave. My husband wants to kill my baby daddy. What the hell have I gotten myself into? Not to mention that damn Chyanne been asking Erica and Brittney about me. For what? I don't know what her ass wants.

Khalil

I had fucked up. I know I say this a lot, but never once had I laid a hand on Pilar, let alone left any marks on her. When she left the room last night I debated on going after her, but I knew it would make things worse. Waking up to an empty house made my blood boil. I don't believe in arguments carrying over to the next day.

When I got to Pilar's job, I saw her talking to some dude. The conversation seemed intense by the expression on her face. As she walked away, he followed behind her, which made me question what the fuck was going on. Once I saw the guard escort him out, I knew it wasn't wise for me to step to him, but I did hear him shout out: "Baby-face, you will see me again! I'ma come see you!"

I hopped out of my car and headed straight for Pilar. So as not to bring drama to her job, I tried to play it cool. After speaking with Pilar, I was livid. She had the nerve to not want to be bothered by me, yet she has niggas popping up at her job? My thoughts were everywhere, "How the hell does he know where she works? Why is he coming back to see her and lastly, who the fuck was he? I had never seen him before and from his attire he wasn't from the city either, or he had to be a square. Pilar definitely has some explaining to do and this funky attitude of hers, better change and change fast.

Pacing the floor all damn afternoon and placing a few calls, trying to find out who this mystery dude was, that Pilar had hanging around, had me exhausted. I was almost ready to go back to her job and scare her into telling me who he was.

Ring! Ring!
"Yo, bro talk to me!"

"His name is Avery. He's from Virginia and he owns a club. He come up here to do business." Tony spoke into the phone.

"Thanks bro, I owe you!"

"Nah, my nigga, I'm good. But check this out, he's having a grand opening this weekend, for his new club. Let's go see what that's about!" Tony urged.

"No doubt!" Khalil spoke sternly, rubbing his hand across his goatee.

"Hey, Kha! You been home all day?" Pilar spoke, starling me as I stumbled forward.

"Yo, bro, I'ma holla at you, aight? One!" Hanging up the phone, I turned to Pilar.

"Why you sneaking up on me? Make a sound next time." Sucking my teeth, letting her know I was annoyed.

"Whatever, Khalil, I don't know why you have an attitude. You're the one who put a bruise on my arm!" Pilar yelled, pointing at her wrist.

"Okay I understand that but, kill all that noise. You think I want the kids to hear you?" Scolding Pilar as if she were my child.

"Liam is on that game and Rue is sleeping." Rolling her eyes, Pilar walked out of the room, slamming the door shut.

I sighed, shaking my head. Things had gone from bad to worst in a matter of minutes. I was going to put the information I had received to great use. Since Pilar planned on hanging out with Jewel this weekend, I would be able to handle this dude, Avery. I wasn't going to approach Pilar until I knew just what I was up against.

Pilar

Khalil thought I was stupid. I was on to him though, picking arguments so I wouldn't go out on Saturday, but I was not going to let him stop my fun. Jewel heard about this club, Onyx. It was the grand opening. I was down! I could use a drink, or a few, for that matter.

"Pilar! Pilar!" Hearing my name being yelled snapped me out of my day dream.

"Yeah, Khalil, what is it?" I said coming down the stairs, "Why are you yelling? Rue is sleeping."

"Someone is here for you." Khalil walked away, ignoring my attitude.

"Okay, who is it?" I responded with sarcasm in my voice.

"Go see! Damn, you ask too many fucking questions!" Khalil sat back, sulking.

"Whatever, stupid!"

Stepping into the living room, I thought I was seeing things. "Hey, Pilar. I know it's a surprise for me to show up unannounced, but it was important." she stated.

"Umm, it's okay, Ms. Edwards. What can I do for you? Is Andre okay?" I asked because of the concerned look on her face.

"Andre is coming along. He was hit over the head with something and suffered a concussion." Ms. Edwards solemnly stated, holding her head down.

Holding my hands over my mouth, I gasped, "Oh my God! Do you need anything? Is he okay, now?"

Now I know, with the history we had, why would I be asking about his well-being, but at the end of the day, we still share a child and I couldn't imagine breaking the news to my son of his father's death.

"He's okay. Andre is home, and he wanted to know if he could see Liam for a little bit this week?"

"Sure, sure. I can bring him to see Andre, Friday, after work." I reassured her.

Reaching out her arms, to me, we embraced and I could tell that the hug made a difference. She loosened-up, some.

"Thank you, Pilar. I know my son has put you through hell but I will always like you better than that hussy Chyanne." She smirked, as she exited.

"No problem, Ms. Edwards. I will give you a call, Thursday morning." Escorting her out, I closed the door and fell into it.

"Why must everything fall on me? I need a vacation and fast but I can't."

Hearing Khalil enter the living room, I couldn't gain the energy to deal with all of his questions.

"So, this nigga know where we live Pilar? How the fuck you allow him to know where we rest our heads?"

"First off, that's still the father of my child and I'm not going back and forth with you, Khalil. He could have died, but I bet you don't care, right? If it's not about Khalil then you will complain!"

"Nah, fuck that and fuck him! He treated you like shit, but now the nigga hurt, you up and running just like a typical captain save a hoe!" Khalil accused.

"Are you fucking serious, right now, Khalil?" My voice cracked. "I can't believe you would stoop that low to say some shit like that. You can get the hell out of my house!" Picking up anything in my grasp I tossed them in Khalil's direction, as he tried to dodge the items.

"There you go bugging out, as usual. You're the dumb ass who wanna help this piece of shit!" Khalil walked away as I stormed in his direction.

"Where you going? The door is that way! Get the hell out my house Khalil! I'm not playing with you!" I latched on to his arm, as he pushed away from me.

"Get off of me, Pilar! I'm not going anywhere! This is my house just as much as it's yours!" Khalil shouted.

"Why are y'all fighting? What's wrong?" Liam asked, peeking outside of his bedroom door.

"Go in the room, Liam!" I pushed him in his room and closed the door. I was not giving up on this fight that easy.

"Mom!" Liam cried, through the door.

"Liam, stay your behind in that room!" I shouted, just as Khalil slammed the door in my face. Pushing open the door, huffing and puffing, I screamed at Khalil, "You got me fucked up! You are going to leave out of my house, right now! I've had enough of your bullshit! You're a jealous, insecure bastard who can't do nothing right but fuck me and fuck me over!" I said, standing up to Khalil.

Pointing his finger at himself and chuckling, Khalil came back at me with, "Who me? Nah, shorty, you got it twisted. That's what Andre is, but if you want that nigga fine, you can have him! I'm out!" Khalil grabbed-up a few items from the dresser. He swatted my perfume bottles onto the floor in the midst of leaving the room.

"Childish ass! Get the hell out and don't come back!" I spat at him.

I fell to the floor, picking up the pieces of the broken bottles.

Peeking back into the room "Oh and by the way, sweetheart, I'm taking my baby with me!" Khalil stated.

Jumping-up to grab the door, before he could close it, he slammed it on my hand. The pain shot through my hand and up my arm so fast, that I couldn't stop the scream of agony that came up from my throat.

"Oh, my God!" I grabbed a hold of my left hand, with my right, to try to stop the throbbing pain.

I wanted to run after Khalil, so that he couldn't take Rue, but the pain stopped me in my tracks, as I fell to the floor. The tears streamed down my face. I looked-up and saw Liam glancing in my direction, before running into his room.

Khalil

Hearing Pilar scream-out in pain, I decided to just leave instead of taking Rue, but I knew the way to get her upset was to threaten her with taking the kids. I had to get out of the house before one of us killed each other. I headed straight for Don's house to crash for the night.

"Yo, bro, I'm coming to crash. Me and wifey had a fight and right now, I'm fucked up over a few things."

"No doubt, I'm here. I told you we was gon' take care of this nigga, Avery." Don spoke into the receiver.

"That nigga, Avery isn't the problem. It's Andre, he gotta go. He almost got hit but somebody half-assed the job!" Khalil boasted. "When I come for that dude, I'm putting him 6 feet under, feel me?"

"Word! Holla at me when you get to the crib." Don said, rushing Khalil off the phone,

"Copy. One!"

Khalil ended the call, pulling over to the side of the street, placing a call to Pilar, only to be sent to voice mail, yet again. Throwing the phone at the dashboard, Khalil was annoyed, "What the fuck?!" He hit the steering wheel, frustrated with all the drama.

"I gotta get my wife and kids away from the city for a bit, while I take care of some things!" Khalil thought, as he started up the car and headed to Don's house.

Pilar

Annoyed was not even what I was feeling right now. Betrayed and torn would best describe what I felt. Picking up my phone, looking at the caller ID flash "hubby", I rejected another call of his.

Khalil had to learn the hard way that I was over all the drama that came with being his wife. Being petty, I unlocked my phone and blocked his number. Something had to give and it wouldn't come from my end this time.

"Who can I call?" I thought, as I heard the tiny whimpers from Rue, over the baby monitor.

"I'm coming baby girl, I'm coming." I said, talking out loud. Once I had Rue settled on my lap, I sat-up in the bed and picked-up my phone, yet again. I had to vent, but I knew Lola was asleep, so I placed a call to Jewel. After 4 rings the voicemail came on. Sighing, I contemplated calling my sisters, but this fight, I wanted to keep to myself.

Placing the phone to my ear waiting on the receiver to pick up, ready to hang up, I heard a groggy: "Hello?"

"Oh, hey! I expected to get your voice mail. I didn't think you would be up for talking." I hesitated.

"It's cool. You know I have no problem hearing your voice."

"I know, but it's late. I just wanted to see if your number was still the same."

"C'mon now, since when do I change my number? I might block you." Chuckling, "But I won't change my number."

"Yeah, well how are you?" I thought if I played it cool, I could hang-up, like the call never happened. What I anticipated to be no more than a 5 minute call, ended-up going on for 2 hours and only ended because Rue needed a changing.

Ending the call and letting out a sigh, I knew it would only get messier, but I needed an ear and tonight I allowed him to offer his...

Andre

Hearing the humming sound on my night stand, I reached over to see who was calling me this late. A smile crept across my face when I saw Pilar's name flash across the screen. I was relieved that my mother was able to get her to agree on me seeing Liam. I was hyped. Once Pilar spoke into the phone, I could hear the pain in her voice, but I didn't pry into it, I just listened while she talked.

"Baby girl, are you sure you okay?" I kept asking. Even though she insisted she was fine, I knew she wasn't.

"I'm fine Andre. I'm just checking on you. I was scared, knowing that I could lose you." Silence filled the phone. "I mean that as you being Liam's dad." She laughed it off.

"Yeah, okay, you know you miss me, shorty." I spoke confidently.

"Boy, please, you know I have my husband, so go ahead with all that!" She chuckled. It had been a long time since I'd heard Pilar laugh. It felt good. If I kept it up, I could win her heart back and get rid of that hot head man of hers.

"In due time, in due time." I thought, as the conversation was abruptly cut-short because of her baby.

"I'll see you Friday, right?" confirming the date. Correcting me, she spoke "You will see US on Friday. Goodnight, Andre"

Relaxing on the bed, my plan was definitely working.

Pilar

I know I was dead wrong for calling Andre, last night, but I had to talk to someone. I kept saying that the call was innocent and it was to check on him, but the nervous laughter said otherwise. I wasn't in love with Andre, nor was I in lust. I was fed up and needed an outlet. Dre just happened to fit in perfectly tonight, but I knew I had to shoot him a text to let him know it was just that.

Pilar: Hey Dre the convo was great but we can't do that again, I'm a married woman and you well you're Liam's dad. Let's just leave it at that, okay

I had to send him the text to reassure him, it wasn't nothing more. The vibration of my phone let me know I had an incoming text.

Andre: baby girl you don't have to explain yourself, I know what it is, and thanks for checking in on me now go get some sleep Ms. Married woman, texting me at 2 am.

Laughing, I couldn't help but reply with a smiley face. Tossing the phone on my nightstand, I snuggled Rue in her co-sleeper and fell out, right beside her.

The rest of the week flew by. Khalil still wasn't allowed home and surprisingly, he abided by my wishes. He sent texts every day, hoping I would change my mind, but I was stern. He had to see that I wasn't joking, this time.

Friday, after work, as I promised, I picked-up Liam to go visit Andre. Khalil didn't know I was going through with the visit. I'll tell him when he comes home, I told myself. On the drive, Liam was quiet. I didn't tell him where we were going because I didn't know if I would change my mind at any time, or if he would tell Khalil.

"Where we going momma?" Liam asked, gazing out of the window.

"On a visit. You will see. It's a surprise." I told him, looking in the mirror, smiling at him.

"Okay." He mumbled, turning his attention back to his iPad, just as we pulled up to the house. I got out and felt the scenery first, before letting Liam exit the car.

"This is a house." He pouted. "This isn't a surprise!" Stomping his feet.

I laughed. "Yes it is silly. Go ring the doorbell, boy." I pointed at the door.

"Fine." Running up on the steps, he rang the bell, until the door finally opened and Andre stood there looking down on him.

"Hey, little man!" Andre scooped him up in his arms. Seeing how his eyes lit up, I knew I had made the right decision by bringing him.

"Hey daddy, I haven't seen you in a long time!" Liam examined the bandage on Andre's head.

"Yeah I know. Daddy was hurt."

Watching from afar, I contemplated whether I should wait in the car or go inside with Liam. Snapping me out my trance, Andre yelled, "Baby girl, if you don't get in here!" Andre motioned for me to come, with his free hand.

"I'm coming." I walked up to the door, as Andre held it for me.

"Thank you." Walking pass Andre, I stopped in my tracks, when I saw a boy sitting on the floor, Indian-style, playing a video game.

"Hi." I spoke to him. The look he gave me could have killed me, if looks could kill. Coming up behind me Andre spoke, "Drew, I know you heard her say 'hi'. What the hell is your problem? I told you about that rude shit." Andre popped him on his head.

"But dad, mom said..."

Cutting him off, Andre threw his hands up. "I don't give a fuck what your momma said. When you with me, you will utilize those manners. Do you hear me?" Andre spoke sternly.

"Yea, dad." Andrew spoke, holding his head low. "Hi, miss."

I smiled at him. "You look just like your daddy."

I looked over at Liam, who had a smug look on his face.

"Baby, what's wrong?" I knelt-down to Liam, so I could talk to him.

"Who is that mommy? Why is he calling my daddy his daddy?" Liam's little puzzled, innocent face broke my heart.

"Well, that is your brother Andrew. I'm sure you two will get along great!" I smiled.

"Okay, mommy." Liam ran off and introduced himself. Andrew didn't take his introduction so lightly, until Andre made him accept Liam as his brother.

The two of them got along great, once the ice had been broken. As I sat off to the side, watching them interact, I was pleased that the visit was going well.

"Come here, baby girl, let me holla at you." Andre signaled for me to follow behind him. Apprehensive, at first, I gave in.

"Wassup, are you enjoying having the both of them together?"

"Yeah, it's great. They have a lot in common and I want Andrew to have his little brothers back, regardless of how y'all women feel about each other."

Giving Andre the side-eye, I leaned in, "Excuse me? Last I checked, you started this drama by sleeping with us both and keeping it a secret!"

I stopped at the dresser, admiring pictures that were plastered on the mirror.

"Listen, I don't want to argue about it. Chyanne knew about you, but I kept it a secret from you. I apologize, but I do want to work on something from here on." Andre sat across the foot board, on the bed, staring at me.

Feeling uneasy, I shifted from one leg to the other. "Well, I'm not arguing either Andre. We have a son together and for the sake of him, we have to be on the same page." I stressed.

"I know. Come here. Why you so far away from me, like I bite?" Smirking, Andre rubbed his hands together, as he licked his lips.

"It's safer over here, Andre. I'm not going there with you." I looked away. "I told you, I'm a married woman, Andre. You have to respect that."

Standing-up, Andre walked up on me, looking down on me, as he closed the door. "And, if you weren't married Pilar, then what?" Andre wrapped his arms around my waist and pulled me close, causing me to lose my balance and fall into him. We both collapsed onto the bed.

"Andre, we can't do this." I tried to push him off. "Stop, okay? My husband would kill me!" I tried to get out of his embrace, but couldn't budge.

"Shorty, stop talking about that lame ass nigga of yours. You didn't walk down the aisle. You called the wedding off, so stop saying 'husband'." Andre pressured me.

I rolled my eyes, "Wrong, he is my husband. We are legally married. We just didn't have a ceremony. Like I said, he's my-"

Cutting me off, his lips covered mine, catching me off guard. His hands roamed my body, as the heat rose. Realizing what was going on, I lifted up off of him and backed away. "Andre what are you not understanding? He's my husband and I love him!" I stared, hesitantly.

"If you say so, but do he love you? That's the question you need to be trying to find out Pilar." Andre shook his head, as he eyed me.

"Listen, Andre I don't have to explain anything to you." Now annoyed, I turned to walk out of the room.

"Well, if he loved you so much, why he still cheating on you? Ask him who Sasha is!" Andre yelled out after me.

I turned to go back in the room, "Excuse me? What did you say? Who the hell is Sasha?" I questioned him, but the blank stare on his face made me want to smack him.

"Ask your 'husband' who she is." Andre said, walking past me.

"F it, this was a huge mistake. Liam let's go." I grabbed up his sweater, letting my anger get the best of me.

"Oh, so now you acting salty? You kill me, you mad at me cuz you with a dog!" Andre sucked his teeth "Typical shit."

"Don't curse in front of my son, Andre." I stated, pulling Liam towards the door.

"Your son? Last I checked, we both fucked each other! That makes me the father, which means he's my son too!" Andre pointed at his chest in frustration.

"Whatever! Liam baby, c'mon let's go. We don't need this negativity."

As I strapped Liam in his seat and slammed the door shut, Andre grabbed my arm, pulling me to the side.

"Pilar don't run away again. I need you!" Andre held onto my arm for dear life.

Pulling my arm away and making myself, very clear, "Get off of me Andre! You are bipolar and I don't have time for this mess. You saw your son, now leave me alone!" Wiggling free of his grasp, I hopped in the driver seat. Andre pulled me out of the car.

"Pilar, stop!" Andre tried to settle me down but I was too fired up. "Andre, you stop! Get off of me!" I yelled, before he covered my mouth.

"Pilar, if you don't hush! Stop all that damn yelling, like I'm killing you." He said in my ear, through clinched teeth.

Nodding my head, I knew I'd better be quiet before he hurt me in front of Liam. I forced myself to calm down. "Okay, Andre, damn, I'm quiet." I stated, yanking my arm out of his grasp. "Crazy ass."

"Pilar, listen, you are stuck with me for life, so you better learn to accept that you had my baby!" Andre explained.

"That's not my problem. My problem is, you thinking you can just touch on me!" Huffing, "You can't touch me. I'm not your woman. Understand that, Andre, and we will be good!" I got back into the car, closing the door in his face.

"Yeah, yeah fix your attitude, before I fix it for you Pilar!" Andre boasted, tapping the car. Rolling my eyes and flipping him the finger I drove off.

"Damn, nut-job!"

I glanced-back at Liam. He hadn't heard a word, or seen a thing. My baby was knocked-out sleep.

Ring! Ring!

I reached for my phone, hoping it wasn't any of the guys in my life.

"Hello?" I spoke, dryly.

I placed the phone on speaker. "Hey, girlie! I'm headed to your house. I hope you are there!" Jewel yelled into the receiver excitedly.

"I'm dropping off Liam and then I'm headed home, hon."

"Well, hurry-up! I need a drink and some girl talk, after your hubby leaves the house!" Jewel giggled.

"Girl, I will update you on all of that. I'm parking the car to drop off Liam now. Gimme 15 minutes, boo."

"Ok girl, hurry!" Jewel shouted into the phone, before ending the call.

I dropped Liam off and hopped on the highway, heading straight to my house. As I pulled-up, I saw Jewel leaning against the door. Before I could fully park, she was at my window.

"Bitch, I missed you! Hurry-up and get your ass out of this car! Let me get a good look at that good ol' baby weight!"

Chuckling, I jumped out, doing my best Top Model stance and turn.

"Girl, you still silly!" Jewel playfully slapped my arm, as we embraced and kissed cheeks.

"Heifer, you looking good too! I see that running every morning is doing that body good or is it the milk?" Slapping her thigh.

"Hell no, this ain't no milk!"

We walked into the house, arm-in-arm. Jewel and I spent hours talking and catching up. She told me about her boo from NYC. I was happy because she would be moving here sooner than expected.

Jewel couldn't wait to see the kids, this weekend and to formally meet Khalil, even though I had filled her in on all the drama. She informed me that every relationship has a rough patch or two, but I was ready to get a divorce and we had only been married for a few months.

"Girl, so you really had a secret damn wedding? I'ma kill you!" Jewel huffed.

"I know. Nobody knew, just my sisters." I exclaimed. "I knew I wanted to marry him, before I brought Rue into the world."

Side-eyeing me, she pressed, "And what if it came out that she was Avery's baby? Then what, my niece would have that fool last name?"

"Well, she came out looking just like Khalil's ass, so I'm good." I laughed, as I searched through my closet for an outfit.

"So, your boo said this party was going to be popping, right?" I questioned Jewel.

"Yes! War said this party is gon be lit! Besides, it's the club's grand opening, so you know it's going to be packed, regardless." Jewel said, deciding on her white romper for tonight.

"So what are you wearing, Miss Thang? I know you plan on wearing some high ass heels, so I brought some as well."

"That's my girl! I'm wearing this two-piece outfit. I'm showing my ass tonight, so you're the designated driver!" I tossed Jewel the keys.

"What?! Why me?" Pouting. "I wanted to drink too!" Jewel whined.

"I need this, Jewel. C'mon, you will be there with your boo." I said. stomping off. She yelled after me as I closed the door to the bathroom, "Fine, cry baby. I swear you're a spoiled brat, Pilar, but you owe me!"

Creaking the door open and peeking out, "Thanks, boo! See, I knew you loved me!" I laughed.

"Yeah, yeah!" She responded, sucking her teeth.

After an hour, or so, we were ready to head out. I caught Jewel giving herself the once over. She had her hair pulled up into a high ponytail, with her white and gold romper, which hugged her boobs and ass perfectly. Complimenting her romper, she wore a pair of Gold Prada pumps and carried a small clutch. Picking up her glass of wine, she sipped it slow, as I walked by, popping her on her ass.

"Ah, nah, shorty, go on with your bad self!" Jewel lauged, glancing in my direction.

I had on a gray two-piece pencil skirt and belly shirt set. Dabbing perfume on the nape of my neck, I pulled my loose curls up in a messy bun and slid on my black Giuseppe's. Placing my hands on my hips so Jewel could get a pic of me, I was happy with how my ample ass sat up in my skirt and my newly perky boobs (due to the milk), spilled out of the v neck top.

"That waist is snatched, bitch! Yassss!" Jewel squealed as she snapped her fingers.

"Heifer, let's go before we have to wait on that damn line!" Glancing back at my reflection, I shook my booty and flicked off the lights.

Khalil

With all the fights me and Pilar were having, I needed something to keep my mind off of her.

"You ready bro? We going to check out this nigga and see what he about." Tony spoke, as he laced up his boots.

"I'm always ready." I pulled my shirt over my head, looking into the mirror, at the bags under my eyes. "After tonight, I'm taking my ass home. I miss my wife."

"Hell, I'm shocked your ass lasted this long!" Tony laughed. "You know y'all like the new Bonnie and Clyde."

"Yeah, but her ass been acting funky for a minute now. But tonight, I'ma go home and bust that ass, real good!" I laughed, stepping into my boots.

"Good, cuz we got bigger issues to worry about." Tony stated, picking up the keys.

"Yea, let me grab my phone and shit and we out." Glancing at the mirror, I noticed the cut on my neck that Pilar had given me, before I stormed out. I missed her and the kids but she wasn't accepting my calls or texts. I hoped tonight I could take my ass home. My damn back hurt from sleeping on the futon in Don's basement.

I arrived at the club a little early so I could get a good spot in the VIP where I could see everything.

"Can I take your order?" I looked up, mesmerized by the beauty standing in front of me. Clearing my throat, "Yeah, yeah get me a bottle of Henny and a bottle of Rose."

Winking at me and licking her full lips, "Is that all, handsome?" She flirted as she reached down to get the menus.

Just then, I spotted shorty coming my way with fire in her eyes
"Yeah, that's all Ma."

Just as she stood-up Sasha walked up on the girl. "So, this is what you do when I walk away?" pointing in the direction of the waitress.

"Girl, if you don't sit your ass down! You nagging already and you just got here!" I sucked my teeth, annoyed that I even started fucking with this chick.

"Whatever, Khalil!" She plopped-down on my lap. "You be thinking I'm playing games with you!"

Shooting her a smug look and setting her straight, "You acting like you my girl though. I done told you about that shit!"

Staring blankly in my face, she complained, "So, what, I'm your bitch?"

Placing my hand up to silence her, I spotted Avery, walk in like he was the man, smiling and giving dap to plenty of people I knew.

"Mutual friends." I responded.

Thinking my plan through, I stood-up, to check-out everything, until the waitress brought back the bottles.

"Honey, c'mon have some fun! Drink this drink I made." Sasha said, raising the glass to my mouth. I gulped-down the concoction. I was ready to sit back down, but Sasha grabbed me towards the dance floor. I wasn't much of a dancer, but the Henny had me ready to bend Sasha over on the dance floor until she got snatched up.

Andre

I stood off in the cut, watching with disgust, as Khalil let Sasha grind her fat ass on him.

"Yet, this is the nigga she marries, tuh damn fuck boy." I said to myself, shaking my head. "He's going to get his. He think I don't know he sent them little niggas to come and take me out. Too bad they didn't succeed at it." Rubbing my hands together as if I was about to eat, I started creeping up on him, to get a better view, but who I spotted, made me fall back.

"Oh, let me wait this shit out!" I pulled the nearest waitress over to order 2 shots of Henny. Gulping down the shots, I stood off to the side. I signaled my 2 boys, in the corner, to keep an eye on Khalil, as I spoke to someone.

"Wassup, playa? It's been a minute." Giving him dap.

"Yeah, it has. I been laying low, but as you can see, I'm back."

I noticed Pilar make her way through the crowd. My dick grew hard at how the skirt hugged her tiny waist and how her fat ass bounced as she walked.

"Damn, my baby mama one bad chick!" I thought.

Creeping in her direction someone grabbed a hold of her arm, stopping her in her tracks.

Pilar

As soon as I saw him, I told Jewel to give me a minute. I had to address him.

"Are you sure about running up on him in here?" Jewel questioned, as I waved her off.

Bending down to snatch up the chick who was grinding on my husband, I was pulled back.

"Pilar, chill! Don't do that here." he spoke into my ear. But the liquor I had consumed had me ready for war.

"Who the fuck is this bitch, Khalil?!" I shouted as I was being pulled away. But, I stood my ground.

"P- Pilar calm down, it's just a-" I slapped Khalil upside his head.

"Fuck you! Once a cheater, always a cheater." I yelled-out in frustration.

The girl he was with decided to speak "Who the fuck are you, putting your hands on me?" she squealed, touching up her hair.

"Mind your fucking business. You just happen to be the trick of the month!" I screamed, spitting in her face.

Khalil grabbed her. "Yo, shorty, chill! That's my wife. You will not disrespect her!" Khalil chastised her as I just watched.

"You got some nerve Kha, but I'll tell you this, come get ya shit and get out my house, tonight!" I turned to walk away, thought about it and took the drink out of his hand and poured it on him.

"You tripping, Pilar!" Wiping his face. I smacked him over and over, until someone put me in a bear hug.

"Get off of me!" I yelled.

"Baby-face, relax!"

I calmed-down, a little and he released his grip. I looked at him, surprised. "What, what are you doing here?" Before I could get an answer I was whisked away.

I was being pulled towards the entrance. "Calm down, baby girl. I got you. You're good." rubbing my shoulders.

I was beyond pissed. The tears welled up in my eyes.

"You're not going to cry. You hear me? You are good. Let me get you out of here!"

Wiping the single tear from my eye, I followed behind him, stopping at Jewel to retrieve my purse and to tell her that I'd see her tomorrow. She was relieved because she wanted to stay with her man anyway.

Reaching his car, I turned to him "I don't want to go home. I want to just get air right now and honestly, I don't want to be alone."

I heard my name being called. I looked up and spotted Andre running out of the club like a mad man. Khalil came out after him, looking around the street frantically.

Sighing, I got in the car and closed the door.

"Thanks Quinn"

Khalil

Shit just went haywire in the club. My wife had caught me, yet again, with a chick and the nigga Avery had the nerve to grab her up. Then, out of nowhere, Que slick-ass escorts my wife out of the club.

"These niggas had me fucked up. Now, I have another body to add to my hit list." I thought. As I ran out, after them, Dre was standing there, at the door, calling out Pilar's name.

"Why the fuck you looking for my wife?"

"Oh she's your wife now, huh? Just a minute ago, you had that sleazy bitch Sasha, all up on you!" shaking his head. "Pathetic hot-head ass nigga!"

I threw my hands up, at Dre and we started throwing hands before the bouncers came and grabbed a hold of us.

"Yo, my man, get the fuck off of me! I don't fucking know you!" I spewed at them.

"You want to fight? Take that shit up the block!" Avery walked out with a set of cops. "These the two assholes who fucked up the opening night!"

Dre shouted, "Nigga you called the fucking cops? What type of pussy nigga calls the fucking cops?"

I shook my head in agreement.

Avery whispered something in his ear.

"The kind whose fucking your baby mama." Chuckling.

I eyed him wondering what the fuck he said because Dre acted like a mad man.

"Yo, I'ma fucking kill you my nigga! Say that shit when the cops don't have me handcuffed, you fucking pussy!" The cops threw us in the back of the car, knocking Dre's head up against the glass.

"Ahh! What the fuck!" Dre yelled, leaning his head back.

Although I hated Dre, I could see he needed medical attention. "Yo, officer, this nigga back here bleeding. He needs a doctor!" I shouted from the backseat.

"Shut-up. He aight!" the officer shouted back.

"Nah, man, he needs a fucking doctor. The nigga head is bleeding!" I continued, looking at Dre. He just held his head down.

"Yo, I hate you, but... But you raised my son, even though you treat Pilar like shit" He laid his head back.

"And your ass treats her better?" I chuckled, "You can't even get playing daddy right!"

"Sorry to bust-up ya little soap opera. Get out!" The officer swung open the door, pulling us out. Dre fell, face first onto the concrete, as I was pushed into the station.

Shaking my head in disbelief, I muttered, "Fuck, this was not how this night was supposed to go!"

Pilar

Falling back into the seat, I let out a sigh, as I gazed out of the window. "I can't believe this happened again!" I chastised myself. "I'm so fucking stupid!"

"Listen, Ma, you're not stupid. I told you, I got you!"

"But, you don't understand Que, I got married to his ass. I pushed out his baby!" I shook my head in disgust, upset that I allowed him to get under my skin, yet again.

"Listen, fuck all that! Come inside and relax." Que grabbed my hand and escorted me to a two-story house that I didn't recognize. Pulling back from him, I inquired "Where the hell are we, Que?"

He found me amusing and laughed "Girl, this is my house. That's why nobody has seen me." He pulled-out the keys and unlocked the door. "I've been laying low."

Following his lead, I stepped into the apartment, removing my shoes.

"Are you hungry? Do you want something to drink?" Watching him walk away I knew exactly what I wanted and it wasn't food.

"Pilar, don't you hear me talking to you girl?" He snapped his fingers, to get my attention.

"Yeah, I hear you, but I just want to get comfortable, if that's okay with you!"

He walked up close to me, taking my clutch and phone out of my hand.

"Mi casa is su casa." He teased.

Laughing, I pecked Que on the cheek. "Thank you, again, Que."

"No need to thank me. Go shower. I'll set-up the guest room for you."

Walking in the direction of the bathroom, I turned to catch him staring, so I gave him a wink. Once I was in the shower, my body became very heavy as I let the tears flow with the water. "How could my life be this complicated?" I thought I was doing everything right!

"Go on a date." Lola said. I shook my head, mimicking her, "Meet someone."

Letting out a slight whimper, I had to laugh to stop the tears from coming.

I must have been in the shower a long time because I started feeling light headed from the steaming hot bathroom. I glided into the room and laid across the bed, wrapped in a towel and dozed off.

Knocking on the door startled me. I jumped up, trying to fixate my eyes on something that I recognized, to remind me of my whereabouts. Everything seemed strange.

"Come in." I said, almost in a whisper, as Que entered with some clothes.

"You fell asleep that fast, girl?" He tossed the clothes at me. I tried to catch them before they hit my face, but I was too slow.

"Why would you do that? You play too much!" I jumped up, throwing the pillow in his direction, as he walked out of the door, knocking him upside his head.

"Close that door, too!" I shouted as he pulled the door shut, behind him.

I threw on the white tee and basketball shorts and headed to the kitchen.

I sneaked-up on Que, as he stood over the stove. "That smells good. What are you making?"

Turning to face me, he smiled. "Steak, sautéed with mushrooms, broccoli and mashed potatoes." Que said, waiting on my approval.

"Umm, I didn't know you knew how to cook." I stated matter-of-factly.

"Well, you were never here, so how would you know that?" Que said looking into my face.

"Well, I'm here now, Quinn. Come here." I held-out my arms for him to meet my embrace.

"Nah, you can't get my hugs. You played me out, the last time I saw you." He said with an attitude.

"So, let me make it up to you, Que." Not waiting on his response, I rose-up on my tip-toes and kissed him.

He lifted me up and sat me on the counter, as our kissing became more intense.

I reached-down and undid his pants buckle. I placed my hand inside his jeans, causing his manhood to jump. He lifted my shirt and fondled my nipples with one hand, while his other hand held onto the back of my neck. Letting a moan escape my lips, I teased his manhood, as I caressed and jerked it, slowly.

"Shit, girl!" He whispered, stepping back. He came out of his jeans and laid me back on the counter, pulling the shirt over my head and removing the basketball shorts.

"Damn!" He stared at my body for a short moment. He then lifted my leg, licking my inner thighs.

Throwing my head back, I moaned, in ecstasy. "Oh, Quinn! God, umm, please don't tease me!" I propped myself up on my elbows looking down in his face, as he glared up in mine, while licking his way to my love box.

"Que, c'mon" I begged.

"Uh-huh." He managed to get out, as he opened my legs and kissed my box.

Hot and ready, I grabbed at him.

"Relax, Pilar, let me take care of you!"

My pouting and rolling my eyes should have signaled to him that I was growing annoyed. I didn't need all of this! I just needed to feel his dick and here he was playing games with me.

Laughing, he returned his lips back to my love box. As he licked and sucked on my coochie, the little attitude I was working up, was forgotten.

Grinding on his face and steadying his head, I moaned. "Umm, wait, you're gonna make me cum!" I panted, as I couldn't hold it in any longer. I began to grind faster as his tongue worked wonders.

"Oh, God, Quinn, ssstop, stop please! Baby, I can't, I can't." I tried to catch my breath, but he was punishing me. Quinn knew what he was doing.

I tightened my legs around his head, trying to hold my pussy muscles together, trying not to cum. "I'm, I'm cumming!" I moaned loudly, as my phone blared from the background. Ignoring it, he continued to lick, until my body shook, uncontrollably. "Uh, Que!" And, then, he inserted his tongue inside me, as I came all over his face.

Ring! Ring!

My phone rang again, as I was catching my breath. Que got up, playfully slapping my leg. "Go get that. Let me clean-up and check this food."

Not really wanting to move, I hopped off of the counter, in a daze. I grabbed my phone. Noticing that it was a private number, I decided against answering it, but my curiosity got the best of me.

"Hello?" I spoke, hesitantly.

"Pilar, are you sleep?"

I was pissed that I had answered the call.

"No, I'm not. I'm still hanging out, why?" I responded, annoyance in my voice.

"Oh, so what, I'm interrupting your fucking fun?"

"As a matter fact, you are!" I spat into the phone.

"Well, I'm locked the fuck up! I called you twice. I need you to come to the precint, Pilar and you need to check on your damn baby father, too!"

I was even more pissed, now. He was ruining the high I was just on.

"For what, Kh.." I stopped short, remembering I was in another man's house. "Why? Y'all got into something that has nothing to do with me!" I shouted into the phone.

"Oh, so it's like that, Pilar? Watch, when I get out!" He spat back.

"Yeah, yeah! I know you not threatening me? Better yet, leave me the hell alone. I'll see you when I see you!" Taking the phone away from my ear, I heard him rambling on, loudly. I looked back and saw Que standing there, in just a tank and boxers. I ended the call.

Khalil

"Baby, I need you right now! Hello?" I shouted into the phone, but Pilar wasn't responding.

"Pilar, are you listening?" Then the line went dead.

I know I had fucked up, big time. Never had Pilar ignored me, let alone hung up in my ear, when I needed her. I wasn't letting my pride allow me to lose my wife. She had stayed through all of the infidelities, what was a dance, compared to that? Pilar didn't know I was fucking her, so I was safe to blame her assumptions.

"No, she didn't just hang up on me!" I thought to myself. I got up from where I was sitting, to talk to the guard. "Yo, let me ask you a question?"

The guard at the desk looked up. "You just did." He was oozing sarcasm.

"Aight, I see you wanna be smart. That's cool, but what's going on with the dude that came in with me?"

"What's his name? Nobody was booked with you." The officer looked at a book and then picked-up the phone.

"Andre, I don't know his damn last name." I told the officer, standing there holding the bars with my face pressed against the cold metal. I waited for his response.

"He was taken to the hospital for medical treatment." The officer said, hanging up the phone.

"Damn!" I looked around. "A-yo, officer, can I make another call?"

"You had your call. Remember, you called wifey?" The officer chuckled, mimicking me.

"Yeah, I know, but I gotta tell wifey about him." I tried pleading my case.

"In a few hours. Go chill your ass down. You gon be here for a while."

Walking off, sucking my teeth, trying not to get under his skin, "Aight, bet." I mumbled.

Sitting back down on the bench, I thought, "Damn I gotta make this shit right."

Pilar

"Sorry about that. Did you make the plates? I want to try that food." I said gliding towards Que.

He tossed the white tee at me. "If you don't put that on, we will not be eating food!" He chuckled.

I pulled the shirt over my head slowly, teasing Que. Rolling it down, I did a twirl and Que walked up on me. "You playing, girl, watch when I bust that ass!" He wrapped his hands around my waist and pulled me in for a kiss.

"Let's eat first. I'm going to take care of you, later." I pulled back, tapping his chest. "So, come feed me, baby. I'm cranky when I'm hungry." I stated sarcastically.

"So am I, but you gave me a taste, so I can hold off for a little bit longer." Grabbing the plates and setting them down on the table, Que pulled out the chair, catching me by surprise, as I grabbed for the chair also.

"I'm guessing you thought I wasn't a gentleman." Que stated, tilting his head to the side.

Trying to disguise my guilt, I said, "No, I didn't. I'm sorry."

I sheepishly looked down at the food. "I'm just not used to that." I admitted.

"Well, baby girl, stick with me and I'll show you the ropes." He said, smiling.

I sat there a moment, while thinking of the 'what ifs' with Que.

"Well, let's eat!"

I erased the thoughts from my mind. How could I think of a future with him when I still had unfinished business with Khalil, Dre and Avery? Sighing, I grabbed the fork and ate in silence. I looked up to see Que staring in my direction, looking pensive. Wiping his face, he excused himself and went to the kitchen to grab glasses.

"Juice, soda or wine?" He yelled out.

Clearing my throat, I responded. "A glass of wine, please."

Finishing-up my last bite, I met Que as he was coming out of the kitchen. He handed me the glass.

"Here, relax a bit. I'm going to shower and then we can do whatever you like." He said, walking away from me.

The tension in the air was thick.

"Can I join you?"

I don't know what I was thinking but I knew I didn't want the night to end.

"If you want. No pressure, Pilar." Que said matter-of-factly.

Walking up on him, I touched him gently, to stop him from walking.

"What is your problem with me? Did I do something to you, Quinn? If you feeling some kinda way, then I can see myself out!" I stomped-off, letting the wine consume me.

"Pilar, stop, listen!" Que said, grabbing my face. "Look at me." He spoke into my face, but I tried to avoid his gaze. "Can you not do this?" He said wiping the tears "I don't want you to do anything you don't want to, that's all, baby."

Looking away, staring out of the window, at the dark blue sky, I reminded him, "If I'm not complaining, then what is the problem? Obviously, I want you Que. I've always wanted you, but I've always had a man, so I held it in."

"You have a husband now, so what makes this so different?" Que asked.

"I'm not happy. I fucked a dude because I was horny and now he's stalking me. My son's father and my husband are beefing." Throwing my hands up, in frustration, I continued, "I'm fucked up. I'm not happy. I've had enough of pleasing people and not myself." Flopping down on the stairs, as the tears fell, I felt pitiful, stupid and lost.

"That's life! So what, you fucked a cornball! Get rid of him and as for them grown men, that's not your beef! You have kids to worry about. Let them go back and forth."

"What about us, Que?"

"What about us?" He asked.

Raising my brow I gave him a smug look. "What do you mean, what about us?"

"Calm down. Not like that. I just said it's no pressure. If it's one night, one month, even a year I'ma still be your people." He pulled me up off of the step. "How long we been down for each other?"

Before I could answer, he placed his finger on my lip. "Come shower with me."

He led the way.

We stepped into the shower. As I looked at Quinn's body, I was amazed and wanted to touch him.

Catching my gaze, he teased, "Uh-uh. Not in here. I want to take my time with you. Wash up."

The next few minutes in the shower were awkward because every time we faced each other, I wanted to touch him.

Following him into the room, I pushed him onto the bed and straddled him. Sliding down onto his manhood, a moan escaped my mouth, "Ahhhh." I grinded up and down, until I had all of him inside of me when something popped into my head, "Condom. Do you have condoms?"

Lifting me up and laying me down, Que went into his nightstand and pulled out a condom. After putting it on, he lifted my leg and inserted his dick inside of me.

"Ummmm!" I looked into his face, as he stared down on me.

"How do you want it, baby?" He whispered.

I bit my bottom lip and threw my head back. "Fuck me, Que. Just fuck me."

He pulled me down under him, palming my ass and lifting me up. I pumped as he fucked me. Switching positions to doggy-style, I arched my back, as Que slapped my ass.

"Throw that shit back, girl!" He pulled me back onto him, as he plunged deeper.

"Oh, Que, I'm about to cum." I half moaned, half whispered.

"Umm-hmm." He pumped faster and harder. I knew he was working up his nut. Pushing me down on the bed, pumping in and out, he grabbed my hair. "This pussy is so good! Damn, baby, I'm about to cum!"

I threw my ass back and tightened my muscles. "Yes, daddy, cum for me." I moaned, biting the pillow.

"Ahhhh!" He yelled out, as his body jerked, letting me know he had reached his climax.

He got up. "Shit, Pilar, that pussy is bomb." He playfully slapped my booty.

I turned to face him, grabbing the sheet to cover myself.

"No wonder niggas is going crazy over your ass!"

I twisted up my lip, throwing the pillow at him. "Really, Que?"

"My bad, shorty." He said laughing. "I'm just saying, though!" He leaned over and kissed me. "I'ma be right back."

He returned with a warm rag for me to clean-up. Afterward, I ran to the bathroom and looked in the mirror. "At least, I used a damn condom this time!" I ran the water and washed-out my mouth.

I came back to Que, lying across the bed. Lying down beside him, Que pulled me in and I passed out on his chest.

Andre

Waking up in the hospital, yet again! I was pissed. Jumping up to head to the bathroom, I realized that I was handcuffed to the bed. "What the fuck is this?"

I shook my arm, not that it was going to become free, but I had to get someone's attention.

"Relax! What's the issue?" The officer rushed to the bed post.

"What you mean, what's the issue?" I asked, raising my arm up to display the cuffs.

With a bewildered look on my face, I questioned him. "You don't see these shits on my arm?"

"Yeah, I see them. They're not coming off, so you better just relax, man." The officer said, steadying my arm.

"What the fuck am I doing here? One minute I'm in the police car, next I'm locked up to this fucking hospital bed! Hell, take me back to the bookings!" I shouted.

2 other officers stood inside the doorway. "Johnson, what's the problem?"

"Nothing. He just came to his senses. He's good, though." Johnson stated, waving off the other officers. "I got this." He reassured them.

"Dre you gotta keep your mouth shut, if you want me to stay on the scene." Johnson whispered, to me.

"Man, fuck that, I pay your ass too much money for you to allow this shit!" I boasted.

"I get that, man, that's why I took over, so I will be a step ahead of them. But, that dude, Avery wants charges pressed against you and that wild boy, Khalil."

I sat up, trying to piece together what the hell had happened.

"Who the hell is Avery and where is Khalil?" I questioned. "Oh, shit, where is Pilar, you know my BM?" Laying my head back, I was still confused.

Johnson shook his head. "Pilar walked away from you and Khalil with that guy Que, who run the courts. Avery is the club owner who threw you and Khalil out. And, well, you know who Kha is. That pretty much sums up the people from the night." Johnson stated. "But, listen, I gotta go. I'ma come check you in a bit." Johnson got up and headed for the door. "Don't do nothing stupid until I get back to your crazy ass, Dre."

"Copy, but, umm, I need to make a call."

Johnson pulled-out his phone. "Hurry up and make it quick and quiet, Dre."

"No doubt."

I let the phone ring out and decided to leave a message "A-yo, baby girl, I know you ain't feeling a nigga, but I gotta speak to you. I'm on lock- down at the hospital and Kha ass locked up. Holla at me, on this line. One!" I sighed, handing Johnson the phone. "She might call you back that's Pilar. Just give her the run-down for me, please." I didn't want to sound desperate, but I was, at a time like this.

Johnson looked in my face. "Aight, I'm doing this for Pilar, not for you Dre." And he made his exit.

Lamont Johnson was my boy from back in the days. When I got locked-up on my first offenses, he was there, as a rookie and looked out from that day forward. I put him on my payroll so that I would be a step ahead of the law. He knew me and Pilar's history, not to mention, he adored her. He always tried to keep her and my son safe that was up until last night, when this new dude popped out of nowhere.

"Fuck! How did she get caught up with Que?" I thought. "Damn, Pilar, you got one hot head, Khalil and now you fucking around with Que, too?" I stared at the sky, out of the window. "How am I going to get Pilar out of this shit? Somebody gotta go and it ain't gon be me!"

Avery

I can't believe this shit. I come up to NYC to open up my new club and these fuck boys tried to destroy everything I've worked for. After seeing Pilar in the club, all the feelings I had for her came out and I had to go speak to her, stopping short when I saw her glaring at a dude.

"Maybe I can see who the fuck her husband is." I thought as I watched her run up on some guy and chick, and jackpot! In the midst of my making my way to her, to defuse the situation, another guy comes and pulls her out of the club.

"Pilar is one popular chick, but I'm going to get her, one way or another."

Having her husband and baby father locked up was just what I needed. It wasn't hard to find her baby father, once Chyanne gave me the run-down on how he played her and how she wanted to get back at him.

"Wassup, shorty?" I said, once she picked up.

"Nothing. It's late. Did something happen?" She said, groggily.

"Your baby father is locked-up. I wanted to be the one to tell you."

"Okay, well, I guess you got what you wanted. But, Pilar does have a husband, also." Chyanne said sarcastically.

"I handled that too, so you should be happy." I boasted into the phone.
"Yeah, okay, so we done here, then?" Chyanne asked, uninterested.

"No doubt. I'll holla." I ended the call before she could say anything else. Envy and greed could make people do the craziest things. Chyanne was just that, she envied Pilar and wanted her to suffer, at any cost. Little did Chyanne know I had a trick for her also. Any woman who could have her child's father put in harm's way was a snake.

I located my laptop and searched for her name. I decided to send her a message:

Avery: Hey baby face, I hope you're ok. I just want to talk, so hit me up.

Keeping the screen open for about 15 minutes, I knew I wouldn't get an answer.

"Fuck!" I knocked the papers off of my desk. "Who in the fuck was that other dude? I hope these guys know I will eliminate all of them to get to her!"

I paced back and forth. I needed a plan. I needed a team. I was determined to make this trip worth my while, since everyone decided to fuck up my opening night. I knew exactly what I needed to do and that was visit Miss Lady, herself.

A smile crept across my face. I rubbed my hands together.

Simple...

Pilar

Popping my eyes open, I frantically looked around the room, patting the bed for my phone, after realizing it wasn't on the night stand. Noticing the other side of the bed was empty, I figured I could hurry and leave before Que noticed. Jumping off of the bed, in search of my clothes, that's when it hit me. Bending-over, holding my head and clinching my teeth, I could barely stand.

"Damn hangover, ugh! Where the hell are my clothes?" I mumbled to myself.

Creeping up on me, Que touched my shoulder, scaring me. "Good morning, beautiful."

Holding my chest, I flashed a phony smile. "Oh, hey, morning!"

I grabbed the sheet, to cover my body.

Que chuckled. "Seriously, Pilar, like I didn't see all of that yesterday." He pointed his finger at my body.

"It doesn't matter. Umm, do you know where my clothes are?" I was still searching for my phone and clothes.

"Going somewhere? It's early. Relax a bit, P." Que cocked his head to the side. "But, if you in a rush, your clothes are downstairs. I washed them and your phone is on the table with your purse." He sat-down on the bed. "You are popular, that phone's been ringing all morning".

I smirked. "Yeah, I have to go. I do have two kids and a husband, not to mention my friend is in town."

He put his hand up to silence me. "A husband?" He chuckled. "So, you going back to him, now?"

"What do you mean, Que? Now you know I'm married and what happened to 'oh, we going to always be people's?'" Cocking my head to the side, I rolled my eyes. "Typical nigga ish!"

"Hold up, shorty, I ain't say nothing. I just thought you would at least take a few days."

I cut him off. "See, that's where you went wrong, thinking!" I shouted. "Don't think when it comes to me, ask and I'll tell you!" I yelled in Que's face.

"What you not gon' do is come up in my spot yelling and shit. Cool, I fucked you, now you can go." Que stated, nonchalantly.

"Really, Que? Oh, that's all this was, huh? Now, you can tell everybody we finally fucked. I hope it was worth it cuz I could have saved the orgasm for someone better!" I shouted, trying to hurt Que.

Laughing and shaking his head, Que just looked on. "Oh, now it wasn't good, huh? You bitches kill me-" Before he could finish the sentence, I slapped him.

"Don't ever call me out my name! Disrespectful ass. You just like the rest!" I stomped off to go retrieve my clothes.

"Pilar! Pilar, stop and listen to me!" Que ran up behind me grabbing me.

"Leave me alone." I pulled my arm back. I picked up my top and pulled it over my head; I bent-down to slip my skirt on. "You are no different, but don't worry, you don't have to worry about me ever hitting you up again!" I glared at him, while I slipped on my pumps. "Where the hell is my phone and purse?"

Que stood there staring at me, pointing toward the island, in the kitchen.

"It's over there Miss Dramatic."

"Dramatic? Dramatic? No, I'ma show you dramatic, cuz y'all niggas got me fucked-up. Like y'all can all say what y'all want and play me, but-"

Que leaned down, kissing me, pulling me into him, as he held onto my waist.

"Shhh! I don't wanna hear all that Pilar. You know I'm not like them lame niggas you used to fucking with, so kill all the noise." He pulled me in closer, as his finger traced my lips.

"I want you anyway I can get you. Go handle your shit and call me later, shorty." Once again, he leaned-down to kiss me. I obliged and kissed him back.

I pulled away. "I gotta go." I headed towards the door. Que followed behind me.

"But, Quinn-" He placed his finger on my lip.

"Shh, Pilar, it can wait. I'm good, so we good, aight?" He popped my booty, as I made my way out the door.

"Que, you drove me here." I stomped my feet, looking around.

"Take these." Que tossed me a set of keys. "Those are to the Range. I'll send my sister to pick it up later."

A smile crept across my face. "Really?" I backed-up to kiss Que on the cheek. "Later, babe." I touched his face, gently. "I'm sorry and thanks for an amazing night." I reached-up and tapped his lips with mine.

"Oh, I know. You just a big baby, but I can deal with that because you are cute when you're mad. Now get out of here, before your husband put out a missing person's report."

Laughing, I hopped in the car and drove off. Just as I stopped at a red light, my phone beeped.

"Hey baby, I'm so sorry about yesterday."

"Don't baby me, miss. You have explaining to do. I'm headed to your house, now." She chuckled.

"Ok Jewel, I'll be waiting for you." Ending the call, I checked all of my messages. The last one caught my attention.

"Pilar, call me as soon as you get this message. If I don't hear from you by the afternoon, I'm calling Ma and dad. Your safety is in jeopardy, baby girl."

Darting my eyes to the clock, it read 11:52am.

"Damn!" Pulling over to the curb, I dialed the number back.

"Hello, hello?" I answered, frantically.

"Baby-girl, where the fuck are you? What happened last night? Who are you around?" Robert rattled-off the questions before I could even answer one.

"Rob, I'm fine. I'm headed home and last night was crazy. Honestly, I don't know much, but I do know that Khalil got locked up and I think Dre is in the hospital, but I haven't listened to all of my messages yet." I sighed, leaving the details of Avery and Que out.

"Bullshit, Pilar. I spoke to your husband and your ass left with Que. Do you not remember that part, or how about some big nigga scooping you up?!" Robert yelled into the receiver.

"Shut up, Robert! I'm sure Kha forgot to tell you that his ass was with a chick too, huh, or did you not know?" I said, mocking him and rolling my eyes.

"He danced with the bitch! So what, Pilar?" Robert stated, nonchalantly.

"Really, Rob? Danced? You know what, I'm done! Now, my husband is your best friend?" I said putting emphasis on husband. "You killing me with all the bullshit! I'm over it and I'm not in any danger, so leave me the hell alone!" I yelled into the phone. Looking down at the phone, I noticed I had an incoming call. "I gotta go." I hung-up in Roberts ear.

"Hello?" I angrily answered.

"Pilar, relax, I've been trying to reach you."

I cut him off.

"Yeah you been trying to reach me so much that you called Robert and told him everything but the truth, Khalil! The fucking truth that you're cheating on me! I don't care though. It's whatever. Leave me alone. Let that bitch go pick your dumb ass up!" I barked.

"Pilar, all these games you playing is getting tiring. I'm not cheating on you, but since we on the subject, tell me something-"

Before he could finish his sentence, I interjected.

"I want a divorce, Khalil, that's what I'm telling you! Now I'm telling you like I told Robert, get off my line!"

"Keep acting cute Pilar. When I run-up on your little ass, I'ma fuck you up!" Khalil shouted.

Looking at the phone and laughing, I put the call on speaker. "You mean if you CAN run-up on me. Did you forget you were locked-up, asshole?" I laughed. "So come fuck me up now!"

"Oh, this shit is funny to you? Yeah, okay, watch when I see you!" Khalil shouted, in frustration.

"Khalil, I mean, my wonderful husband, who wants to kill me, I have to go. I have a dance waiting for me!" I mocked him.

"Pilar, don't fucking play with me!" And that's when I ended the call.

I listened to the rest of my messages. I heard Andre speak into the phone. After hearing his message, I wanted to reach out, but I was over all the drama for one day, so I decided I'd deal with him at a later date.

As I pulled up to my house, I could see Jewel, standing there, leaning on her car, on her phone.

"Sorry I'm late." She lifted her finger to signal meto give her a minute.

I unlocked my door and removed my pumps. Running to quickly change my clothes, I heard my phone ringing from the other room.

"I hope it's nobody annoying on this other line." I sighed, picking up the phone.

"Hey, baby!" I smiled and spoke into the camera.

"Hi, mommy. What you doing?" Liam spoke into the camera as he walked through my mother's house.

"I just got up, baby. What are you doing and where is Rue?" I asked trying to locate where in the house he was.

"Grammy feeding her and I'm playing with my toys."

"Oh, okay. Are you having fun?"

"Yes! I love you, mommy!" Liam shouted.

"I love you too, baby. Liam, why are you moving so much?" I asked, looking into the camera. My question was answered, seeing my mom's face appear on the screen.

"Hey, Ma." I smiled

"Don't 'hey' me, girl! I have a few words for you, but first, say 'hi' to your baby girl." My mom spoke dryly, as she lifted the iPad to show Rue's face.

"Hi, mommy's little girl! Hi. Baby! Let me see that smile."

Hearing Rue coo into the camera and watching her smile, melted my heart. "Her so pretty! Yes, she is! Mommy loves you, and yes, I do!" I spoke to Rue until my mother spoke.

"I'm calling you in a minute. You better answer, Pilar Monroe! Do you hear me?" My mother spoke in a stern tone. All I did was nod my head.

I looked-up as Jewel was coming through the door. I plopped-down on the sofa. Jewel tilted her head, looking at me curiously.

Just then, my mother called back.

"So, mom, why are you acting like I did something wrong?"

My mother cut me off. "Pilar, I want you to listen and listen carefully to what I'm going to say." Carol reprimanded me.

"Okay."

"Did I raise you to be running around here like you lost your mind with all these guys? I thought you walked down that aisle because you loved Khalil, but then, I hear you hanging with two and three other guys like you some sort of whore!" Carol shouted into the phone. "I never get in you and Khalil's business, Pilar, but you're acting like you have no sense. I'm not babysitting my grands so you can go and fuck the next guy!" She raised her voice!

"But mom that's not what-" She cut me off.

"I thought I said I was talking and you were going to shut that mouth of yours and listen? Did I not say that, Pilar?"

I didn't answer. I was too afraid to get chastised again.

"So now your ass can't answer? Don't make me come to 2461, Pilar!"

"Yes, mom, I hear you." I sighed and rolled my eyes.

"Now, I want you to tell me what the hell happened and why is your husband and baby father locked up! And, don't be slick and leave out them two other guys, that thug Que, you know Tiffany's son and whoever that other guy is." Carol stated.

"Ok, fine." I placed the phone on speaker and called Jewel over to the island, where I was now standing.

"I'll tell you everything, but mom, you can't judge me, okay?"

"Since when have I ever judged you, Pilar? Tell me the story because me and my belt is ready. I think you forgot what an ass whopping is. Well, I'll remind you quick!" I looked over at Jewel. She was laughing.

"I went out to this club opening, which happens to be run by Avery. Wait, let me go back. Khalil and me haven't been on good terms, all week, mommy. He bruised my arm because I found out he wanted to kill Andre, right? Well, last year, I went on a date with a guy, Avery and it just so happens that it was his club that was opening. So, I end up there. Khalil was dancing with some chick and I ran up on him."

"For dancing with someone, Pilar? It's a damn club." Carol said

"No, mom, I know it was more than that, but when I hit him, Avery came and tried to hold me down, that is until Que-" (blushing as I said his name) "Que came and I left with him. Mom, that's all, I'm home and I'm fine." I said, cutting-out half of the story.

"Stay the hell away from Que. He is a thug and you have enough going on as it is with Khalil and Andre." Carol chastised.

"Fine mom, fine, but Jewel is here, so can I catch up with her, please?" I pleaded.

"Yeah, but I tell you this, if Robert calls me again with your nonsense, I'm sending him and your father after you."

Widening my eyes, I asked, "Mom, but why? Forget it, okay? I'll be good." I ended the call with my mother and turned my attention to Jewel.

"Avery is going to be a problem, Jewel. He wants to keep dealing with me! Thank God he didn't know that he could have been Rue's father."

Jumping up off of the stool, Jewel grilled me. "So, he doesn't know about the baby and Khalil doesn't know about him, Pilar? Girl, you are one sneaky ass!"

"Sneaky? Do you think Khalil would have stayed if he knew? I'd like to keep Avery and his 'could have been' ass, a secret!" I glared at Jewel.

Raising her hands, she quipped, "Your secret is safe with me, but you know what they say, Pilar."

"No, what do they say, Jewel?" I rolled my eyes at her.

"What's done in the dark, will soon come to the light." She stated, as a matter of fact.

"Well, I'll wait to deal with that." Getting up off of the stool, I was eager to quickly change the subject.

"So, what's our plan for tonight?"

Khalil

Pilar has rejected another one of my calls. I was vexed and needed to get out and get to my house, to deal with her but here I was locked-up.

My thoughts were interrupted. "Khalil Taylor, you are released!" The officer shouted.

I jumped-up, feeling relieved. "Yes! So I don't have to go to court?" I asked as I reached the desk.

"No, the charges were dropped." The officer stated, handing me my belongings.

"Copy." I turned to leave, but turned back. "So, what about ole boy I was with?"

"Charges dropped, as well."

I walked-out of the building, breathing-in the fresh air. Sasha was waiting in my black BMW. Sucking my teeth and mumbling, to myself, "Her ass the reason I'm here now".

I tapped on the car, "Wassup? What you doing here?" I asked.

"Damn, baby, it's like that? I'm glad you're okay." Sasha exited the car, reaching for a hug.

"Nah, I'm not even doing that. You the reason I'm here, Sasha." I said, pointing at her.

"Really, Khalil, what did I do but dance with you?" Sasha asked with her hands on her hips.

Don was in the back seat laughing.

"You find something funny, cuz I don't?" I asked, leaning into the back seat. I was annoyed with Sasha and waved her off.

"So you're going to ignore me Kha, huh?"

I was pissed-off that she called me what Pilar calls me. "Shut the fuck up! Stop calling me Kha and second if your dumb ass didn't get smart with my wife I would be good!" Pointing in her face, I spoke through clenched teeth. "But, no, you want her to know I fucked you!"

"Oh, so you worried about your wife feelings now? We been fucking for 3 months. You haven't complained before. She must have finally gave you some!" Sasha chuckled.

"Whatever, bitch, you can bounce. I'm done fucking you!" I spoke calmly. "Now, I'ma drop your ass off and we're done."

"Fuck you, Khalil. I don't need you or a ride. You'll be crawling back to me." Sasha walked away from the car to hail a taxi.

"Dumb bitch." I mumbled, shaking my head.

Don hopped into the front seat with me. "I told you she was crazy. Now, she gon' really tell Pilar y'all been fucking."

"She do and I'll have no problem knocking her off!"

"Okay gangsta!" Don laughed.

"You find something funny, motherfucker? As a matter fact, I'ma just go to the crib so I can shower and shit."

"Your crib, with your wife?" Don stared at my face. "Cuz I think you just might as well kill yaself!"

"Nigga, shut-up! I'ma handle wifey!"

"If you say so! You and I both know Pilar. She gon' tear your ass up, but I warned you!" Don chuckled.

I already knew going home was going to start a war, but I had some things to run by Pilar and get my wife back on my team. I had other shit to handle, like this nigga Avery.

Pulling up to the house, I noticed Pilar's car in the driveway. "Great!" I thought, cuz I had a bone to pick with her.

Unlocking the door, I heard giggling. Sucking my teeth I thought, "That's why she was being cute, showing off as usual." I tossed the keys on the island. Don plopped-down on the couch.

"Listen bro, she got company, so don't be going in there spazzing!" He shouted as I walked away.

"Yeah, yeah!" I replied, waving my hand.

I reached the bedroom door and swung it open, just as Pilar was modeling a dress.

"Hey, Khalil." Jewel greeted me.

"Wassup, shorty, how you?" Eyeing Pilar as she rolled her eyes and sashayed pass me.

"I'm good, just visiting for a few." Jewel stated.

"That's wassup, so what trouble y'all got into?"

"Cute, that's my girl, you really think I'd say shit about any trouble?" Jewel glared at me, smiling.

"If y'all did, I'll find out" I said, walking towards the master bathroom.

"Well, that's what you gon' have to do." Jewel stopped and suddenly backtracked. "Hey, Khalil, I don't know much about what's going on, but go talk to your wife, before you leave."

"I'ma do just that." I reassured her.

Jewel got up and left the room, closing the door.

I knocked on the bathroom door. Pilar ignored me.

"Pilar, let me holla' at you" I shouted through the door

"For what? "Go be with your bitch!"

"C'mon Ma, kill the noise. Just open the door." I knocked on it once more, just as she unlocked it.

"What?" She spat, staring at me, as she leaned against the sink.

"Really, P.? C'mon now, that bitch not nobody but more importantly who was that nigga at the club? Nah, better yet why was you with that dude Que?"

"Oh you got questions? Tell me how long you been fucking the bitch and I'll tell you who the dude was."

"Alight, well-"

Pilar waved me off. "Before you lie to me, Kha, I know you fucked her and more than once, so you better come correct!"

Thinking, "Damn, now how the fuck I'ma lie, now?"

"I only fucked her three times. Cut her off, yesterday, so-"

"Fuck you! You're a liar, but don't worry cuz, trust me, I'm done with your trifling ass!"

Pilar pushed pass me as she went to the dresser to retrieve clothes.

"Pilar, what the fuck you mean you're done? You better put those clothes back and sit your little ass down! Shit, I don't care if you sleep in a separate room, but you're not leaving this house!" I shouted, grabbing up her clothing.

"Put it down, Kha! You think I'ma sit around and let you continue to play me? I'm not stupid. You got what you wanted, a baby, so now, go be with your bitches!"

She grabbed at the clothes in my hands and we started having a tug of war.

"Pilar, you think that's all I wanted?"

"That's all you're good for, being a good dad! Fucking bastard!"

Pilar tugged the sweater as I pulled at the other end. Finally, she let go, causing me to lose my balance.

"Take it cuz your bum bitch needs it more than I do!"

Grabbing some leggings, Pilar rushed out of the room and into the hallway, to take off her dress and put on the leggings she had in her hand. She flew down the stairs in a bra and leggings, as I ran after her.

"Jewel, get my sweater off the island and let's go!" Pilar shouted. Reaching the bottom of the stairs, Pilar was greeted by Don, coming up.

"What are you doing here?" Pilar asked, covering her exposed breast with her arm.

"Coming to save you from your angry husband." Don said, turning his back to Pilar. "Where you going with no shirt, anyway?"

Ignoring Don, she yelled to Jewel, "Let's go!"

She slipped on her loafers, by the door. She grabbed the sweater from Jewel, putting it on and zipping it as she pulled open the door.

"Pilar, if you leave this house, I'ma fuck you up!" I shouted after her, as Don tried to hold me back.

"Man, relax. Let her cool off." Don stressed.

"Nah fuck that, she bugging the fuck out. I'm beyond tired of her shit yo!" brushing passed Don as she pulled off.
"Yo just take ya shower and come back to the crib for a few days"
"She better go get my kids I know that" pulling out my phone placing a call to Tony.

"Wassup?" Tony answered on the first ring.

"If you see that nigga, Que, let me know. I gotta holla at him." I said, frustrated.

"Copy."

Ending the call, I headed to the master bathroom.

"I'll be down in about an hour, so chill out." I said to Don.

"No doubt." Don replied, tuning on the big screen.

I sat on the bed, thinking to myself. "What the fuck is going on? Is my wife really ready to call it quits?"

Looking at the room that was in shambles, I was annoyed by how things had gone with Pilar.

"Fuck!" I shouted, tossing all the clothing off of the bed. After sitting in silence, for a few minutes, I jumped up. "Nah, I got to fix this shit. But, first, let me hit this shower."

Andre

As I pulled up to my house, all I could think about was getting into a hot shower, fast.

Walking through the door and looking around, I noticed none of my mother's things were there. I thought, "Good, some peace and quiet."

Heading upstairs, my phone beeped, notifying me I had an incoming text.

Pilar –Hey! I'm sorry. I'm just checking my messages. I hope you're good. One!

Smiling, I was relieved it was her texting me

Andre -wassup baby girl I'm good but holla at me I need to talk to you in person

After sending the message, I knew I wouldn't get a response to us meeting up. Pilar was avoiding me and I knew it was for the best, but with all the drama that was going on, I had to see her.

Pilar - are you home? I can stop by really fast.

Andre - yea I'm here I'll leave the door unlocked come over

Pilar -be there in 10 mins :)

Placing my phone on the dresser, I didn't wanna seem pressed, but getting her to agree to meet up with me was an accomplishment. Jumping into the shower, I let the water just fall over me. I was lost, trying to piece everything together. I had not only lost my baby mama, but Khalil was seconds from losing her ass also. After about 20 minutes, I hopped out and threw on a tee and basketball shorts.

I walked up on Pilar, as she looked at the picture of us on my television stand.

"Hey, baby girl." I whispered in her ear, as she jumped. Turning to face me, she popped my arm.

"Boy, are you crazy, scaring me like that?" She half smiled and half frowned.

"My bad, I thought you heard me come up behind you." I said, looking her over. "What the hell do you have on?" I scrunched-up my nose at her outfit.

She rolled her eyes at me. "Shut up, Dre. I just grabbed the first thing I saw and left."

I laughed. "I can tell! Why were you rushing?"

"Khalil wanted to argue and me," She said, pointing at her chest. "I want a divorce."

"Yeah, yeah! Your ass not divorcing him, so stop yapping those lips!" Looking down on her, I could see the seriousness on her face.

"I'm serious, I'm done. I can't believe I even went through with the marriage. Like, I'm just over it. I can't, I can't!" She sobbed, shaking her head side to side. I just grabbed her and held her.

"Listen, mama, it's going to be aight. Don't beat yourself up, over it."

I was holding her and she leaned in, on my chest.

Finally, speaking, I could hear the cry in her voice. "No, you don't understand. I'm tired of being fucked over!"

Backing-up, she looked up at me. "First, your ass hits me, then leaves me with a kid. I meet Khalil and his ass can't keep his dick in his pants and then Avery-" She chuckled.

I saw the deranged look on her face. Trying to ignore her rant, I rubbed her arms.

"Don't touch me. All of you are dogs or looney! Date somebody and you will feel better. Fuck outta here! I feel worse!" She hung her head, as she plopped-down on the couch.

I stood there looking at her, like she was crazy. "Relax, because you're scaring me".

Jumping-up, suddenly, Pilar paced back and forth in front of the couch. "I'm scaring you? Do you not think that I'm not scared?! Do you?!" Pilar shouted. "I have a looney guy who won't let me go. I fucked-up and my husband, my husband is going to kill me once he finds out I had sex with Avery and not only that, but I ended up pregnant with Rue and I didn't know who the father was, until I pushed her out!"

I stood there, in shock. "Bingo! So that's where that nigga comes into the picture."

"I need a drink. I need a whole fucking bottle. Andre I'm outta here! I just told your ass everything!"

As she brushed pass me, I grabbed her arm and pulled Pilar in.

"Listen, you're not going anywhere and if you do, I'm calling Khalil!" I tried calming her down, before she did something irrational.

"Call my husband? You don't even like his ass, but you gon, call him? Wow, Andre!" She pushed off of me.

"You're damn right. You are losing it and I want to talk to you!"

"Talk about what Andre, huh? You wanna talk, then talk! What the fuck!" Pilar shouted.

"If your ass shut up, I can talk." I shouted back, shaking my head out of frustration. "You need to stay away from Que. I don't know what your ties to him is, but you need to leave his ass where you left him."

She cut me off. "Oh, please, Dre-"

I put up my hand to stop her, midsentence. "If you want to stay out of trouble, stay the fuck away from him, Pilar!"

I let the anger in me rise, as I spoke. "You're so fucking hard headed! First, you got your hot-head husband looking to beat your ass and then you go around and get mixed up with Que, the dude who can't seem to stay out of the hood." I shook my head. "You're so smart, 'til you're dumb!"

"Whatever! Nobody runs my life and don't worry about what I'm doing with Que. As far as you talking about my husband, one thing for sure is, he doesn't hit me!" She waved her finger in my face. "You were the women beater, or did you forget?" Cocking her head to the side.

"No, I didn't forget, but since you wanna be a smart ass, coo,I I'm done!" I headed towards the bar. I needed a drink because Pilar was pissing me off.

She walked-up behind me. "Don't walk away from me and dismiss me Andre! This is not over!" Pulling my arm so I'd face her, I just smiled. Pilar was so sexy, especially when she was having one of her many tantrums.

"Do you hear me, Andre? Like, I'm so tired of y'all niggas!"

Just as Pilar turned, to walk away, I pulled her in, kissing her deeply. As her body tensed up, I backed away.

"What are you doing, Andre? Are you crazy?" She looked at me, bewildered.

"Yeah, I'm crazy. Crazy for letting you walk away." I held onto her hand, as she tried to get out of my grasp. "Pilar, just listen to me for once. Stay away from Que and that nigga Avery will be taken care of."

"Whatever, Andre. I'm out. I have to go." Pulling her hand back, Pilar opened the door. Before walking out, she looked back at me with a slight smile and waved.

"Later, baby girl. Be safe."

Watching her walk out the door was hard because I wanted my family back. I know that's how it always goes, but I needed her close to me. I knew what I needed to do and that was to befriend her again.

Pulling out my phone, I saw I had a missed call from a number I didn't recognize.

"Hello, who is this?" I said into the receiver.

Pilar

Sitting in my car, in front of my mother's house, I was lost in thought.

"I can't believe I'm beefing with my husband, kissing my baby father and sleeping with Que. I know I said I wanted to date, but that was before I got pregnant and married". Shaking my head. "Now, was not the time to get caught-up in nothing. That damn Lola! I don't care, I'm blaming her because she's the one who put me up to dating."

I pulled-out my phone. I decided to give her a call.

"Hey, sis!"

"Wassup, sis? What you doing?" Lola asked in a cherry voice.

"Sitting in my car, thinking how taking your advice on dating got me in some drama."

"Hell no, you will not blame me for your shit! What have you gotten your ass into now?" Lola shouted into the phone.

"Come out with me and Jewel tonight and I'll tell you!" I suggested.

"If you don't meet any lames on my watch, I'm down!" Lola laughed.

"Ain't shit funny, girl. I'm not trying to meet not near another dude!" I protested.

"Good, cuz you don't know how to just date! No, you gotta have sex and end up pregnant!" Lola busted out laughing.

"F, U Lola, that's not funny!" I said pouting into the phone.

The beeping in my ear made me realize I had another call coming through. Looking at the receiver, my face lit up. "Lola, let me call you back" I said, rushing her off the line.

"Okay, cool." I switched-over to the caller.

"Hey, hon." I cooed into the phone.

"Wassup? I didn't expect you to answer. I was just going to invite you to Miami, in 2 weeks."

I contemplated if I should go. He sensed my hesitation and spoke-up. "Before you decline, you can bring your girls as well."

"Sounds like fun. I need some fun, so I guess I'm down!" I said, smiling while I checked myself out in the mirror.

"Don't be guessing, shorty. But, good, you can come pick up the money for your tickets and I'll book the beach house for y'all."

"Now, you know me better than that. I can pay for my own ish, Quinn." I protested.

"I never said you couldn't, Pilar, but if I'm inviting you to Miami, it's my treat!" Que responded.

"But Que-" He cut me off.

"Listen, Pilar I don't wanna hear it. Let a nigga treat you, without you being all Ms. Independent!"

"Okay, fine, Quinn, but next event is my treat." I quickly said.

"Nah, you good Ma! I know this gon' be the only time I get to have you for a full weekend."

"Yeah, okay Que." Looking up, I saw Jewel coming towards the car carrying Rue. "Hey, babe, let me call you back, I'm about to pick up my babies."

"Do your thang Ma, I'll text you the info." Que said, ending the call.

Smiling and hopping out of the car, I embraced Rue. "Hi, baby!" I said, kissing her chubby cheek.

"Your mama is mad at you girl, so you better have a good excuse as to where you been." Jewel warned me.

"What you mean?" I asked with a bewildered look. "I spoke to her already. Better yet, she spoke to me, remember?"

She nodded her head and pointed. "Oh, you didn't notice your husband's car?"

"Damn, what is he doing here?" I sighed.

Shaking my head, as I walked to the door, I heard my mother's voice.

"That better be Pilar Morgan Taylor walking through the dam door!" Carol yelled, questioningly.

I looked-over at Liam, who was laughing. "Something funny, Liam?" I asked him, as he nodded his head.

"You in trouble, mama!" Liam said, as he hugged my leg.

"Give me a kiss, I'll handle Grammy." I said, walking into the kitchen. "Hello, mother. Do you really have to yell like that?" I asked, sitting in the chair.

"You better be glad that's all I did was yell, Pilar." Carol said "These games you're playing need to stop, Pilar!" My mother glared at me.

Avoiding her gaze, I played with Rue.

"Look at me, when I'm talking to you, Pilar!"

"Yes, mama." As I looked-up, I noticed Khalil standing in the doorway, behind her and rolled my eyes in his direction.

Caught off-guard, my mother popped my lip.

"What was that for, Ma?" I shouted, grabbing my mouth.

"You're grown but you're not too grown to get popped, Pilar. You know better than to roll your eyes at me!" Carol walked over, taking Rue from me.

I was pissed. "Ma, I didn't roll my eyes at you. I rolled them at my damn husband!" I tried reasoning with her.

Turning around, Carol saw Khalil smirking at me. "Khalil you wasn't going to make your presence known?"

Clearing his throat, he stammered, "Uhh, yeah, I was Ms. Carol, but, umm, you-" She waved her hand, cutting him off.

"Save it, Khalil! Y'all better fix this shit, now!"

"Ma, there is nothing to fix!" I protested, standing up.

"Oh, yes the hell there is! I will not have your husband calling me, talking about your disappearing acts, again!" Carol stated, cocking her head to the side. "You both wanted to get married and married couples work shit out, not disappear when things get rough!" She said, glaring at me.

"But, Ma, walking away is easier than dealing with Khalil!" I pouted. "I will not stay with no damn cheater and you shouldn't want me to!"

Khalil jumped in. "I didn't cheat on you, Pilar. You think you know, but you don't have proof"

"Proof?! Proof?! Are you serious, right now, Khalil? I don't need no damn proof I know when my husband is cheating. Let's not forget that this isn't the first time, so I'm well aware!" Fed up, I let my anger get the best of me and started airing out the drama me and Khalil were having.

"That's the past, Pilar! You said you were pass that shit, yet every chance you get, you throwing it up in my face. Tell ya mama who Avery is!"

"I don't have to explain nothing to my mama, cuz I didn't bring it to her attention. Your punk ass did!" I shouted, startling Rue because she started crying.

"That's enough! The cheating has got to stop! If y'all cheating on each other, just get a damn divorce!" Carol reasoned.

Rolling my eyes and grabbing Rue from my mother, I walked away. "There she goes, running away, as always!" Khalil protested.

"I'm walking away because I want a divorce!" Removing my ring from my finger, I sat it on the counter as I left out of the kitchen.

"Pilar! Pilar!" My mother called after me.

Ignoring her as I continued to walk, I bumped into the last person I wanted to see.

"You don't hear Ma talking to you, brat?!" Robert stopped me in my tracks.

"Who you calling a brat? You gon stop all the name calling!" I rolled my eyes in his direction, brushing past him.

"Pilar, Ma is calling you! So, you just gon' be disrespectful, huh?" Robert said in disgust, turning his nose up.

"What's the issue, here?" My dad questioned the two of us.

"Dad, its Robert, always acting like he's someone's father. I'm leaving though, so don't sweat it!" I said sitting Rue in the bouncer.

"C'mon, Jewel." I said, signaling our exit.

"We leaving the kids?" Jewel questioned.

"She will not leave them babies and she bluntly disrespecting me. Do I look like a fucking baby sitter, Pilar?!" Carol shouted out in anger.

Sucking my teeth, "I never said you was a baby-sitter. Their father is here, he's taking them." I challenged back, not expecting what came next.   Robert smacked my face.

"What the fuck is wrong with you?! I told you I'm not your child so don't fucking put your hands on me!" Swinging my arms in his direction, Roger grabbed me up.

"Relax, Pilar!" He restrained me.

"Get off of me! Everybody always grabbing on me and not this woman beating motherfucka!" I shouted, huffing and puffing, scaring the kids.

"Roger, let her go! Don't hurt her, baby!" Carol said picking-up a crying Rue.

"I got her, Roger." Khalil walked up on Roger, tapping his arm.

"You don't have no one. Don't nobody fucking touch me!" I shouted, breaking free of Rogers grasp.

"I know you better stay over there, Pilar!" Robert warned.

"And if I don't, Robert? Trust, you will get dealt with!" I glared at him and picked-up my bag. "Liam, let's go!" Walking over to my mother, "Can I have my daughter?" I asked, reaching out my arms.

"Pilar, you need to calm down. I'm not letting these kids go with your ass today." Carol stated. "Liam, baby, go ahead in the room."

Putting my hands on my hips, I replied. "Oh, now I can't take my kids, but just a minute ago- You know what? Never mind, I'm out." I turned to walk away and Khalil grabbed at me. I jerked back. "I want a divorce. I'm not repeating myself, again."

Falling into my driver seat, I started up the car. Jewel came flying out of the house. "Chick, you are not going anywhere, alone." Waving her hands in front of the car. Smirking, I unlocked the door. "Where the hell do you think you going alone? Not in this frame of mind." Jewel smacked my thigh.

"I don't know where I'm going, but I know I'm not staying home." I sighed, pulling off.

"We're getting a room and we are going to have a relaxing night." Jewel stated.

"I guess." I said, not looking in Jewels direction. "Let me stop by my house and grab up a few outfits."

"Do your thang, baby girl. I'll be out here in the car."

Upon entering my house I headed to the bedroom to pack some clothing and shoes. Stopping at the mirror, I finally got a glance of my face.

"What the hell?!" I screamed-out, noticing the red mark on my cheek and my busted lip. Touching my stinging cheek, I grabbed my makeup bag.
"I'll need to make a miracle happen." I said, talking to no one in particular. "I'ma relax

tonight, but I swear I'm so over this nigga and the extra drama!"
The tears began to well up in my eyes as I stared blankly at my reflection...
Grabbing my phone, I sent a text.

Pilar: hey I really need y'all tonight. I'm getting a room tonight. I'll text y'all the address as soon as I check-in.

Pressing send I grabbed up my duffle bag and exited the house, not looking back.

Pulling up to the block, I looked around at my surroundings. An eerie feeling came over me, as I stepped out of the car.

"Yo, my man, let me holla at you for a minute!"

I turned around, patting my sides, realizing that I was naked. I hesitated, until I heard the voice again.

"What chu looking for?"

Turning to face him, I spoke-up. "What's the problem, Dre? Why you rolling up on me, like a snake?" I said staring him in the face.

"Kill all that! I wanna run something pass you, Que." Andre stated, standing in front of me.

"What do we have to talk about?"

"I'ma ask you this one time to stay away from Pilar. You're trouble and if my son's mother gets hurt messing around with your ass, I put that on everything, it's not going to be a happy ending for you!" Dre dropped it.

"First off, don't come to my hood threatening me and second Pilar is a grown ass woman. She does what she wants. I want all y'all fake-ass goons to stop approaching me, when Pilar can make decisions on her own." I responded back, as I walked away from Dre.

"Yeah, aight! I warned you!" Dre walked off.

I was pissed-off that I had gotten caught slipping in my own hood. I could have laid it out there, that me and Pilar were fucking, but that's a cornball move, so I kept quiet. Pulling out my phone, I placed a few calls to let everyone on this end know if they saw Dre, Khalil or Robert lurking, to send them my way. After I checked in on the hood I decided to call Pilar myself.

"Hey." Pilar spoke dryly into the phone. I took the phone from my ear to check if I dialed the right number.

"Hey, babe, what's wrong? Why you sound like that?"

"Nothing, Quinn. Wassup with you?"

"I need to see you, Ma."

"Quinn I can't, not right now. Can you talk to me over the phone?" Pilar stressed.

"Nah, Ma, what I gotta tell you has to be face to face, but since you too busy Ima holla at you, shorty."

"Okay, Quinn-" Before she could finish, I ended the call. I knew I was acting salty, but the thought of her being busy just after we had kicked it, fucked my head up. I told myself she was married and this was all fun and gam, but I had let old feelings surface. Stopping my train of thought, I looked down to see Pilar calling me back. I rejected the call and placed her number on the 'block' list.

"Now, she gon' do things my way." I mumbled, hopping into my car and racing to the diner, to get something to eat.

Walking in, I placed my order to go and sat on the stool, thinking I had to get everything in order, before things spiraled out of control. Glimpsing in the mirror I thought I saw a ghost, "Chyanne". I turned around to get a better look, and damn right, it was Chyanne, sitting next to a familiar face.

"Sir, your food. Hello, sir?" The waiter said, snapping me out of my thoughts.

"Uhh, yeah my bad. Here, keep the change." I said tossing a $20 on the counter.

"Damn, that's the dude from the club, but how the hell does he know Chyanne?" I wondered.

Chyanne

Spotting Que at the counter, in the diner, I just knew my cover would be blown and everyone would know I was back in the city.

"Shit." I mumbled.

"What's up girl, why you cursing?" Avery grabbed my hand into his.

"Que. Que saw me. He's gon' tell Pilar I'm back in the city and if he does that, she will be out for my head, before I can creep up on her ass."

"Listen, I'm sure Que is harmless. Didn't you say they stopped fucking with each other?" Avery asked, concerned.

"Yeah, you right. I'm good, but the way he looked at me was like he was thinking something." I stressed.

"Girl, you acting paranoid. How you plan on getting to Pilar, if you acting scared already?"

"Oh, I'm never scared, nor pussy, so you can quit while you're ahead, Avery."

"Copy, but let's get out of here. I wanna show you a good time, like I planned." We got up from the both, and I pulled-out my phone, following behind him. Checking my Instagram, I logged into the fake account and searched

Pilar. I wanted to see what she had planned for tonight and if I could make my move on her.

Turning around, Avery snatched the phone out of my hand. "What are you doing? I was talking to you!" He stated.

"Give me my phone back, Avery. I was texting, damn!"

Looking down at the screen, Avery looked shocked. "You stalking Pilar?" Avery asked.

"How would I be stalking her, if she added me, Avery? Think about it." I snatched my phone back from him, moving ahead of him.

"Where you going?" Grabbing my arm as I swatted his hand away.

"To go get my son from his grandmother's."

"Fine, but we haven't even talked about anything."

"Babe, I'll call you later. Matter fact, I'll come by your room, tonight." I said, running my hand across his chest, causing his manhood to jump in his pants.

Holding my hand, pulling me close, he whispered, "Now you know I'm not going to let you leave me like this." We both eyed his growing manhood.

Sucking my teeth, I was annoyed that I had started him up. "So, drive me to my house, Avery." I suggested.

I hopped into the passenger seat. Avery stared in my direction. "That's why you my boo, now."

I rolled my eyes. "Why Avery?" Asking, but not really concerned with his answer.

"Cuz, you down to fuck a nigga on demand!" He hyped-up, hitting the steering wheel, pulling off.

I stared out of the window, thinking I was not going to his damn room, so let me just get it over with now.

I looked in Avery's direction, while he looked at the road, placing my hand on his zipper to undo it and exposing his semi-hard dick.

"Damn, baby, you can't wait, huh?" He slowed-down, positioning himself comfortably enough for me to remove his dick, without rubbing it against the zipper. Leaning down, spitting on his manhood, I positioned myself to place the tip on my lips. I licked and sucked the tip. The car swerved, a little, before he gained control of the wheel. Placing one hand on my head, he pushed my head down.

"Shit, girl, you gon' make me cum." Gaining control of his hand, on my head, I deep throated and gagged, causing him to let loose pre cum.

"Bingo! I was almost done." I thought, as I bobbed my head up and down.

Pulling-over on a back street, Avery grabbed the back of my head, shoving his dick down my throat. I gagged and he pumped faster.

"Oh, bay, I'm bout to cum!" He moaned.

His manhood jerked, letting me know that he was at his climax. Lifting my head and jerking his dick, he squirted cum all over my face and hand and his pants.

He laid his head back, eyes closed. "Shit, girl, why you do that to me?"

I opened the glove compartment and grabbed tissue, wiping my hands and face. I reached in my purse, pulling out hand sanitizer and mouth wash. After cleaning my hands with the sanitizer, I poured mouthwash in my mouth, opened the door, gargled and spit.

He wiped himself off with the tissue and zipped-up.

I looked at Avery, with my nose turned up. "C'mon, we don't have all day. Drop me off at my house. I gave you what you wanted, Avery." I said, slapping his forearm.

"Alright, so you letting me in or what?"

"No. That's all you get today, playboy. I gotta go get my son."

"Aight, aigh.t" Avery said, pulling up to my building. I stepped out of the car and Avery got out to walk me to the building, but I stopped him.

"Listen, I don't need an escort."

"Okay, then, Ms. Gangsta. I forgot who I'm dealing with."

Blowing him a kiss, I entered my building and walked to my door. Pulling out my key, I felt a presence behind me. I was pinned up against the wall, as I turned.

"Welcome back, missy!"

My eyes popped, as I noticed who it was.

"What do you want?"

"I want you to stay the fuck away from Pilar. If I find out you have anything to do with anything happening to her, it will be your last day breathing!" And, just like that, Robert left.

Andre

"Yo, I need to holla at you on some grown man shit." The caller said, into the phone.

"Copy, so speak."

"Nah, I need to meet up with you tonight, for the sake of Pilar. Hell, she the mother of our kids."

"Nah, you right and I wanna get back at that nigga Avery." I said enraged, thinking about him.

"And, I wanna holla at Que. So, the feeling is mutual."

After Khalil ran off the address to where he wanted me to meet him, I got dressed. Not really trusting him, I grabbed a gun and placed it in my back. Yeah, I know, we want revenge but he was just the enemy not too long ago.

Pulling up to the building, I leaned up in my seat, over the steering wheel, making sure I was at the right spot. The street was dark and it was quiet.

"See, I knew this nigga was up to some funny shit." Starting up my car, Khalil appeared in front of it holding up his hands.

"Yo, where the fuck you going, Dre? I told your ass the building on the corner."

"Nigga, this shit looked like a fucking set up. I wasn't going to get caught slipping!" I yelled out of the window.

"My nigga, I told you already, my beef ain't with you, as long as you don't put your hands on my wife or disrespect her." Khalil walked to the driver side.

"Yeah, aight, copy." I hopped out of my truck, following behind Khalil, checking my surroundings as we entered a building. It was dark, with just one light shining. Peeping around the corner, expecting to see a group of guys, I noticed there was just one dude, in the corner. A wave of relief came over me.

"So, this is it, just us three?" I wasn't naive, but I was treading lightly, not to set his hot head ass off.

Turning to face me, as he pointed to a seat, Khalil spoke, "Yeah, it's just us. This is personal, so I'm not involving a lot of niggas."

Nodding my head, I responded. "I dig it."

Sitting down, I noticed the dude staring in my face. Khalil peeped the grill, as he picked up a bottle of Henny.

"Yo, Tony relax. This dude ain't no threat, but that nigga Que is looking at a death sentence." Throwing back the shot of Henny, Khalil passed the bottle my way.

"Nah, I'm good." I wasn't about to get caught slipping, cuz at any given moment,

Khalil could hit me and I wouldn't be able to fire back.

"Pass it this way." Tony suggested.

"Speaking of Que, I ran into the nigga earlier and he played tough like I was sending empty threats to him about fucking with Pilar." I boasted.

"Say no more. Now, I did some digging on Avery." Khalil pulled-out a piece of paper, passing it in my direction. Looking over the paper, it had everything laid out on Avery Steller. He is the owner of a club called The Spot, located in Virginia. He has a 13-year old son, with a woman named Sariya, who is a store manager, in his hometown. It had his address and the address of the hotel, where he stays here in NYC.

Displaying a big smile, I was satisfied with the information. "Thanks I appreciate this. I'ma use this to my advantage. I don't have much on Que, yet, but when I do some research-" Khalil waved his hand.

"Don't worry about it. My wife will lead me right to him. Pilar is a rookie at this shit and a good woman. She gon' slip-up soon." Khalil said, confidently.

"You know her better than me, so I'm sure you can handle it." I said, reaching for a glass, as Tony slid me the bottle. Raising my glass, Khalil lifted his and Tony next, as we toasted to getting rid of these useless motherfuckers.

After a few hours, of talking shit, we had finished a gallon and a half of Henny. I learned that Khalil and Pilar were beefing and she hadn't stayed home, since the incident at the club. Khalil had been caught with Sasha, who popped outta nowhere, hot and ready. What fucked up my head was when he told me that he thought Pilar fucked Avery.

Pilar was my good girl and the thought of her fucking someone other than her husband, made my blood boil. Hopping up from my seat, I gave them dap, as I stumbled to the door. Looking back from the doorway and lifting my fist in the air, I said to them, "We gotta do this again."

"Yo, you good?" Khalil joked. "You can't handle the brown." They chuckled.

"I'ma big boy. I got this. I'ma holla."

Sitting in the driver's seat, I contemplated my next move...

Pilar

Looking down at my vibrating phone, I decided I'd check the messages, once I got in the hotel room.

"You okay hon, or you want me to give you some space?" Jewel asked, as we rode the elevator upstairs to the room.

Staring off into space, I just nodded my head. I was drained and didn't want to talk about it, until everyone was together.

"Yeah." I sighed, opening the door to the suite. Tossing my bag on the floor, I walked pass the Living Room and laid across the first of the two Queen-sized beds, kicking off my shoes.

"I'ma start the shower for you and fix us a stiff drink, since we won't be getting stiff dick tonight!" Jewel poked out her lips, causing me to laugh.

"Oh, I just may leave your ass for some!" I winked.

"No, you will not!" Jewel walked off into the Living Room, as my phone vibrated again. Realizing I had forgotten to check it from the previous messages, I picked it up.

Group chat: Sissy I hope you're okay. I can't make it out tonight. I'm sorry, it's Darius birthday and we are hanging out. :(-Mia

Frowning up my face I sucked my teeth, go figure I thought, placing my attention back on my phone to finish reading

Group chat: hey boobie! Let me know where you want me to meet you, I can stay out a bit but I'm not staying the night

Pilar: thanks Tasha I'm staying at the W hotel suite 1609, Mia it's cool I wasn't aware of it being his birthday... Enjoy!

After going back and forth, with my sisters, Jewel came to let me know my shower was ready.
"Hey, Jewel, if Lola texts me let me know, please." I said opening the bathroom door.
"Sure." Jewel went into the Living Room to the bar, to see the selections of liquors that were available.

Stepping into the hot water eased the tension that was in my shoulders. Relaxing and adjusting to the temperature, I placed my face under the running water and ran my hands through my hair. "I could stay right here, forever." I thought to myself.

I know I was wrong to cause the drama at my mother's house, but nobody knows what I'm going through, or seem to care. Seeing Khalil at my mother's house threw me for a loop, because she never butted-in too much, giving her advice.

He had cheated one too many times and I needed to get away from him for a while. No one seemed to be looking at that.

Yeah, I shouldn't have slept with Que, but just like Khalil found his way into the bed of another woman, I have to live my life, as well. I definitely have to get my life in order. If I don't do it, then, who will?

Getting married, just for the sake of being married, was a bad move and I'd be damned if I stay around looking stupid, once again.

Hearing a knock on the bathroom door, I shouted over the running water, "Yes, wassup?"

"Your damn phone is blowing up!" Jewel yelled back.

Opening the glass door and sticking my head out, I asked, "Well, who is it from?"

"Random number, Lola and some other people including your mama!" Jewel said, scrolling through the calls.

"Aight, see what Lola said."

I emerged from my revelry in the bathroom, and stepped into the Living Room wrapped in one of the W's luxurious body towels, as Jewel read Lola's message.

"She said she can't hang-out tonight, sorry." Jewel turned up her nose. "Bullshit."

I laughed at Jewels facial expression. "Okay. Call my mama back and tell her that I'm okay, but that I'm sleeping."

"Sleep? Girl, I'm not lying to Ms. Carol."

"Are you serious? I had to lie to Ms. Debra plenty of times for your fast ass!" I said stepping over to her and snatching the phone from Jewel's hand. "I'll just call my own damn mama!"

Jewel giggled, walking over to the bar and leaning against it. "Miss Thang, don't think I didn't notice that hickey on your thigh." She winked at me.

Looking down at my thigh, I frowned. "Dang, I'ma kill Que! What if my husband had seen that!?"

I called my mother back to find out she was just checking up on me. I flopped-down on the sofa, marveling at the luxury of the room!

"Where are the stiff drinks you was raving about?" I said grabbing a pillow and placing it in front of me, as I sat cross-legged on the white sofa.

"Yours is in the freezer. I'll get it!" Jewel jumped-up off the Chaise Lounge by the floor to ceiling windows, sprinting to the kitchen area.

Handing me my drink, Jewel grabbed her bag "I'm going to shower. I'll be back!"

"Cool." I responded, sipping the drink. I twisted up my mouth. "What the hell is this Jewel?"

"You like it?" Jewel asked, from the bedroom.

"Too damn strong!" I said, eyeing the glass, as though I could decipher the ingredients.

"Good, now I'll see you in a few!" She responded back.

Sitting on the sofa, gazing out on the lights of the city, I took another gulp of the drink. I pulled-out my phone and checked my email.

Staring at the screen, I couldn't believe Avery was still trying to contact me, after I had told him to leave me alone. And, then, the club event made things even worse. Shaking my head, in disgust, "Looney bin." I decided I wasn't going to play tag with him, so I didn't respond. I placed the phone to my ear, to return the many calls.

"Hey!"

"Hey." He answered, groggily.

"I'm sorry I woke you. Is everything okay? You called me."

"Yeah, I was just checking up on you. I know you been going through it, shorty."

"Oh, okay. I'm fine, but get some sleep. I'm headed to bed, as well." I lied to rush Dre off of the phone.

"Aight, shorty, night!"

"Night." Ending the call, I scrolled through my call log to a few missed calls from Que. Before the phone could ring, he answered.

"Hello?"

"Well, let the phone ring next time, scaring me half to death!"

"What do you want, Pilar?" Que asked, agitated.

"Oh, you still acting salty? If that's the case, why did you call me?" I asked, regretting even making this call.

"Don't sweat it, go be busy, Ma! As a matter of fact, I got somebody coming through, so I can't even talk, right now. Holla!" Que ended the call before I could respond.

Looking at the phone, I sucked my teeth. "Oh, he getting too familiar with this hanging up in my ear. Cool, it is what it is." I thought, as I tossed my phone. I knew the rest of the random numbers was from Khalil, so I didn't even bother returning them.

"What you thinking about?" Jewel snuck up on me, scaring me.

"Just these dudes! Que is mad cuz earlier, I told him I was busy, now he has a chick coming to his house and then Avery ass still stalking me, not to mention my cheating-ass husband." Sighing, I grabbed the glass and finished the rest of the drink, in one gulp.

Jewel reached for the glass "Okay, that's enough. You had enough to drink, girl."

Pulling my hand back, displaying the deuces sign, I laughed. "Uh, no you don't. You said we needed stiff drinks, so I'll be making glass number two. Where is your concoction?"

"Okay, fine. You're right, but Pilar, it's going to sneak up on you!" Jewel warned.

Instead of taking heed to her, I went to the refrigerator and poured another glass of whatever it was. I finished the second glass, in record time.

Stumbling over to the chaise, I laid back, letting the alcohol consume me. After a few minutes I sat up! "Jewel, do you know how much shit I put up with? I took the beatings from Andre, the cheating from Khalil, I met Avery and he's a damn looney who's obsessed with me and now, Que! He wants to act like a jealous boyfriend and we are not even a couple!" I shouted at the ceiling.

"Okay, calm down Pilar. I know it looks bad, but what you need is to be by yourself, girl!" Jewel tried reasoning with me.

"No, I'm going to Que's house, cuz he is not going to fuck me, then play me like some thot!"

I jumped-up off of the chaise, and ran the bedroom, in search of some clothing.

Jewel grabbed my arm, trying to calm me down.

"Pilar, your ass is drunk and you will not be going anywhere drunk!"

I pulled away from her. "Fuck that! I'm not soft! I'm tired of this shit and one of them is going to get it. I don't care which one it is!" Pulling up my jeans and pulling on a shirt.

"Girl, relax your ass!" Jewel popped me on my cheek, snapping me out of my crazy rant. "Relax, Pilar." She pulled me down onto the bed.

"Listen, if you wanna go over there, baby girl, you are not going alone and you need to calm down before we roll up on him." Jewel rubbed my arm.

Looking up, at her, I smiled because I knew Jewel was my ride or die chick. I had doubted her a few minutes ago.

"Okay. I'm calm, I'm calm." I repeated, getting up, grabbing my sneakers.

"Good, now let me get dressed!" Jewel proceeded to the bathroom, as I sat staring off into space.

The drive to Que's house seemed to be dragging. I continued to call his phone, but all I got was his voicemail. Sucking my teeth, after what seemed like the 10th call, I threw my phone on the dashboard and rubbed my face.

"What the fuck?!" I startled Jewel, as she swerved on the road.

"Listen, crazy girl, you wanna have outbursts, at least, warn me. I'm kinda tipsy and you breaking out in rants!" Jewel shouted.

Ring! Ring!

My phone started blaring. Noticing it was Tasha, I grabbed it.

"Hey, sis!" I spoke into the phone.

"Where the hell are you?!" Tasha shouted into the receiver.

"Driving to Que's house." I whispered into the phone, embarrassed.

"Bitch, what the fuck are you doing, going to see Que when you just texted me you needed me to come to this hotel? Never mind, Pilar, I'm going back home and when I see you I'ma kill you!" Tasha yelled into the phone, chastising me.

"No, don't go Tasha. Can you take a cab to me and Jewel? We need you to drive us back to the room." I said into the phone.

"Have you lost your mind-" Before she could finish, I interjected.

"Please, Tasha? We had drinks. Well, I had more than her and Jewel had enough. By the time you get here, I'll be finish with Que." I pleaded.

"I swear, you better be glad you are my baby sister! Give me the damn address!" Tasha sucked her teeth, then hung up.

Pulling up to the block, I told Jewel she could wait out in the car for Tasha, while I went in the house and if I wasn't out by the time Tasha got there, to come get me. Jewel agreed because she was exhausted.

"You sure you wanna go in alone? Matter of fact, I'm going to call you, in a few minutes. If you don't answer, I'm coming in."

"It's cool. If I'm not out by the time Tasha come, then you can panic. I'm good." I said.

Walking up the block to the house, I noticed his bedroom light on, so, I knew he was home.

"Thank God!" I spoke to myself, as I rang the bell and then knocked on the door. After a few more knocks, the light in the living room came on.

Moving the curtains in the window, to the side, to see who was there Que opened the door.

"Pilar, what the hell are you doing here?" Que questioned, standing in the doorway.

Letting my anger take over me, I pushed him into the house. "What you mean, what am I doing here? You haven't answered my calls and you been acting funny after you get some pussy from me, like I'm some slut from the block!" I poked Que's chest, as he backed-up.

"Relax, and stop fucking poking me. Yeah, I ignored your ass, cuz u acting funny, like I'm some nag. I don't have time for the 'I love my husband', then next minute 'I hate my husband'." Que said, grabbing my arm. "Make-up your fucking mind, Pilar!"

"Make up my mind? What the hell happened to, 'Oh, I'ma take it how I get it' bullshit?" Cocking my head to the side, not really expecting an answer. "That's exactly what it was, bullshit! Now, you wanna act like a bitch and start crying? Man the fuck up! Niggas cheat every day, so, don't get in your feelings, cuz I said I was busy!" I shouted, breaking free of Que's grasp.

"Really, Pilar? What the fuck is going on with you? You smell like you been drinking. Sit your drunk ass down, cuz this ain't even you talking!" He emphasized, pulling me to the couch.

"Yeah, I had some drinks, cuz dudes like you make me want to drink, stressing me out over nonsense. I wasn't with my fucking husband, but if your ass didn't hang up on me, you would know what I was doing!"

Throwing my hands in the air and walking towards the door, I spat at him. "I thought you were different. Maybe I need to stay with my cheating-ass husband, than to even deal with your punk ass!" As I grabbed the knob to leave, Que grabbed my hand, putting his other hand around my waist.

Whispering in my ear, he said to me, "Listen to me. I can admit a nigga got tight, but I don't want you to leave."

I turned to face him, my face streaked with tears.

"I shouldn't be here. I need to go." Pulling away from Que, to open the door, he pulled me back in to his chest.

"Pilar, stay with me. We can get pass this misunderstanding. I'm sorry, baby girl."

Looking up into his face, I saw the sincerity, but I was exhausted with everything that came with cheating.

"I gotta go." I patted his chest. "I'm sorry for sleeping with you, Quinn."

"What do you mean, sorry? Listen, Pilar, take this envelope and think about the trip." Que said, grabbing the envelope, off of the table.

"I will." Snatching the envelope, from his hand, I walked out the door, just as Tasha was coming towards the driveway.

"Heifer, get your ass in this car, now!" Tasha signaled towards the car. Chuckling, I nodded my head.

"Yes, mama." I said sarcastically.

"Seriously, Pilar? You drag us all the way out here?"

Rolling my eyes and cocking my head side to side, being a bitch, I asked her, "Are you done?"

"Don't make me fuck you up, Pilar! As a matter of fact, no I'm not done!" Tasha said, mushing me towards the car.

"Don't touch me, Tasha. I'm not playing with you!"

"I don't care if you're playing or not. I'm tired and you wanna be Ms. Drama Queen, as always. Dad told me the scene you caused at the house, too!" Tasha said, reaching for the car door.

"Scene, I didn't cause no scene! They are all just crazy and expect me to put up with the nonsense." I said, speaking up in my defense. Reaching for the passenger door, I decided against sitting next to Tasha.

"Jewel, get in the front." I tapped her leg, waking her from her slumber.

"Huh, what?"

"Go sit in the front with Tasha, I'm not in the mood to be scolded by my older sis!" I mocked.

"Whether you in the back or front you gon' hear my mouth Pilar. Your ass need to get it together, and quick!" Tasha shouted from the front seat. When we were secured in our seats, she pulled off.

"Whatever, Tasha! Y'all act like I'm the only one with drama." I said turning to look out of the window.

"You're right, you aren't the only one with drama, but you bring the most and you welcome that shit with open arms, dragging everyone else in it with you!"

Looking in the mirror, I caught her glimpse and rolled my eyes.

"So, then, stay away from me. You don't have to be around it."

I turned my attention back to the window, ignoring her. Yeah, I know I had enough drama in the past year, to last a lifetime, but everyone has drama. I just couldn't get a break. I didn't know how, but I planned to get a break, real soon...

Khalil

After my wife had walked out of her mother's house, angry, pissed me off. This shit had really gone too far. I needed to find my wife. I needed to really fix this shit, but I didn't know if I should do it tonight or just let her chill. If I left her alone tonight, she just may end up with some next dude and I wasn't having that, so after toying with the idea that Pilar could be entertaining another dude, I got up in search of my wife.

I watched Andre leave, then Tony followed behind him. I jumped-up, developing a plan, in my head. This had to be fixed and fast. Hopping into my car, I tried her number again, which was another failed attempt at reaching her. I checked our joint account for recent transactions. I could never find her by this, but tonight was different. My eyes bulged, as I stared at what was charged.

"Oh, hell no! Pilar got me fucked up!" Staring at the phone again, I was enraged. "She must think I'm going to let this ride! Nah, baby, not a room!" I banged on the steering wheel, talking out loud. "Baby, please tell me your ass is alone in that room or I swear I'ma kill you and him!"

Shaking my head from side to side, I pulled off, on my way to the W. Letting my anger get the best of me, I started thinking of every dude that Pilar could be entertaining and that's when he popped into my head.

"Yo!"

"Yo! I was seeing if your drunk-ass had made it home, in one piece." I chuckled, trying to disguise my anger.

"Oh, yeah, I told you my man, I got this. I'm not new to this shit!" Dre spoke into the phone.

"Copy, copy, well, I'ma holla."

"No doubt." Ending the call, I was relieved that Pilar didn't back track to her baby father. Pulling up to the hotel, I self-parked, instead of using valet parking and headed straight for the front desk.

"'Scuse me, miss?" Slurring my words, in hopes that this tactic would work.

"Hello, sir. Can I help you?" The woman at the front-desk smiled, politely.

"Uhh, yea." I patted my pockets, as if, in search of a card-key to the room, that I didn't have. "Me and my wife booked a room and I'm kinda drunk, so I don't remember nothing." I staggered to the side a bit, stepping back.

"Okay. Can I have your name, sir?"

"Taylor, the room is under Pilar Taylor, my wife." I leaned on the counter. "I did say I was married, right? She a lil sexy one too! I'm a lucky man!" I chuckled while the receptionist checked the database. After showing her my ID, she said: "Suite 1609, sir, on the 16th floor."

She directed me to the elevator, after I assured her that I could find it.

"I lost my card-key and my wife gon' be mad I'm just getting in." I winked at her. "You can't get me an extra card-key can you?" I licked my lips, flirting enough to get what I needed.

"Mr. Taylor, normally, we only give two card-keys maximum, for security reasons, but I know the feeling of sneaking-in, so I'll make an exception for you." As she punched information into the computer, I smiled inside. "Here you are, Mr. Taylor!"

I staggered a little as I turned the corner to where the elevators were just to keep-up my game of being drunk. I stepped on to the elevator and inserted my card-key to get to the 16th floor. "Jackpot! Pilar better not be fucking around on me!" Opening the door slowly, so as not to get caught, I noticed it was dark, save for the city lights, coming through the huge windows.

"Pilar! Pilar!" I whispered, but no answer. Finding my way to the bedroom, I walked over to the bed. I patted it. "Empty." I used my phone's light to check the room. "Shit, it's empty." Looking around, I found 2 glasses and women's clothing thrown on the bed. "Okay, so maybe she's not with a dude, but why the second glass, then?" I thought, as I peeked in the bathroom and went back into the living room area. Coming up empty-handed, I was pissed, until I heard Pilar's voice on the other side of the door.

"I don't care. You don't have to speak to me. Hell, you can leave if you want to!" Pilar spat out.

Shutting off the light on my phone, I quickly ran into the bathroom and hid behind the shower curtain. "Damn, now I feel like a chick, snooping on my wife." Hearing the door opening and close I held my breath. I heard more female voices.

"Fuck you! You're a big ass baby and trust I'm outta here in the morning!" Tasha spoke.

"Do y'all really have to fight again? My head is killing me. Fuck, shut-up, Pilar!" Jewel yelled out, frustrated.

"No! She starting shit, as always!" Pilar fired-back, entering the bathroom and closing the door.

"If you wasn't running the streets with-"

Pilar pulled back the curtain and nearly passed out. "AHHH, WHAT THE FUCK!" Pilar shouted, falling back onto the toilet.

Shit, I missed what Tasha had said, looking at Pilar, holding her chest as she sat on the toilet.

Someone banged on the door.

"You okay, Pilar? Pilar, answer me right now!" Tasha yelled.

Catching her breath, Pilar managed to spit-out, "Oh, you care about me, now?" Pilar stared in my face, as her chest heaved up and down. "I'm good."

"Pilar, I can explain. I was worried." I stepped out of the shower, grabbing her hands. "I'm sorry, I scared you." Snatching her hand back, she slapped me.

"I deserve that." I admitted.

"You deserve more than that! What are you doing here, Khalil?" Pilar asked, with a bewildered look.

"Khalil?! What is Khalil doing here?" Tasha shrieked.

"I was snooping, sis! My bad, I scared y'all" I shouted through the closed door.

Pilar stood-up, stepped away from me and pointed to the door. "Get out Khalil! Get out, now!" She shouted. "You have lost your fucking mind, spying on me!"
"Your ass cut your phone off and you left your mother's house pissed! You think I wasn't going to come looking for you?" I yelled back, standing in her face.

"I told you to leave me alone. I want a divorce. First, you cheat and now, you're spying on me?" Pilar asked, shaking her head.

"Listen, P., I just said I was sorry. I was worried sick about you." I said, trying to pull her in, but she backed away from me, throwing her hands up.

"I want you to leave me alone, Khalil. I'm so serious! I've had enough of the infidelities!" Pilar looked into the mirror, giving me her back.

Looking at her up and down, I walked up on her, placing my hands on her waist, as I planted kisses on the back of her neck.

"Khalil, stop!" She squirmed, trying to get from under me, but only succeeded in turning around to face me. I placed both hands on the sides of the sink, so she couldn't leave. "Kiss me, Pilar and stop fighting it."

"Get off of me, Khalil. I'm not up for your games! Get off!" She pushed me in my chest. I pinned her to the sink and kissed her deeply. Wriggling, she managed to turn her ass to me, once again. "Umm, Khalil, stop! I'm serious! I don't want to do this!"

My hand roamed up her shirt to her breast. I massaged her right breast, taking her nipple and squeezing it, knowing it was going to set her off. Pilar leaned back, on me, breathing heavily. A smile crept across my face because I had won, yet, again.

"Pilar, I love you. I fuck up from time to time, but I do love you." I whispered into her ear, as I slipped her out of her jeans.

"No, you don't. You don't love me, you just love fucking me, Kha."

I didn't want to lose my hard-on, with her talking shit. I pulled her thong to the side and slid inside of her.

"Shit, Khalil!" Pilar moaned, as I fucked her. She threw herself back on me.

"Umm, hmm baby, take this dick!" I pulled her hair while I continued to fuck her.

"Ahh, ahh, Khalil, I'm going to cum!" Pilar shrieked. I placed my hand over her mouth, so her cries of pleasure would be muffled. Glancing in the mirror, I saw Pilar staring back at me with sheer pleasure on her face, making me work up to my climax. Bending her over, placing both of my hands on her hips, I pulled her in, as I reached my climax.

"Kha, I'm cumming!" She squealed, in a hushed voice. Feeling her body jerk and her muscles contract on me, I came in her.

"Damn, Pilar! I've missed that shit!" I whispered in her ear, planting kisses on her neck. Sliding out of her, I stepped out of my jeans and turned-on the shower.

Pilar gave me her back, as she searched for something to cover herself.

"Pilar, why you giving me your back like I'm some stranger? I'm your fucking husband!" I said in frustration.

Pilar continued to ignore me, as she reached for a wash cloth off the rack. Wrapping the towel around my waist, I walked up on Pilar. Spinning her around to face me, I noticed the tears on her face.

"Baby, c'mon don't cry! I'm sorry I've hurt you, but I want you to come home. I need you to come home, P." I pulled her in to me. She cried into my chest. I allowed her to stay there while she just let everything out.

"Khalil, why is this happening? I can't understand why you cheat repeatedly!"

Lifting her chin up, so I could look into her eyes, I told her, "Baby, listen, I can't go back into the past, but I can make everything right from here on out."

She pulled away from me, saying, "No, Kha, that's not good enough. You continue to say that and guess what?" Cocking her head to the side, she said sternly. "You fuck-up, so don't tell me you will change!"

"P., listen, I know I've done some fucked-up shit, but do you think I would be creeping over here if I didn't love you?" I asked.

"Yes, cuz you're used to me coming back, Khalil! Every single time!" She emphasized. "I'm not doing it this time! I want out! I can't continue to be unhappy!"

"So, why the hell you just fucked me? Answer that, Pilar?"

"Because I wanted to see if I would regret divorcing you!" Pilar shouted. "But as much as I love you, Khalil, I love me more!" She stepped into the shower, leaving me to let what she just said marinate.

"Aight, Pilar, I'm out then!" I grabbed my belongings. "I'll shower when I get home!" I shouted over the running water.

"Uh-huh." Was all that she said.

Jewel and Tasha just stared at me, as I walked pass them, sitting in the living room.

"Wassup?" I said, giving them a chin-up, as I walked out the door.

"Hey!" They answered in unison.

The drive home was draining, as I went back and forth in my head, on what my next move would be.

For the next few days, I stayed with Tony because Pilar was giving me the cold shoulder, when I did come around. To avoid Liam asking questions, I just kept my distance.

"Yo, Kha man, Que's boys is around the corner talking about we can't be on this end."
"What?! Who the hell is saying that?" I asked jumping out of my Range Rover.
"Ralph and Dominic." Don pointed pass me towards The Courts. Looking back, over my shoulder, I saw Que approaching them and looking in our direction.
"Yo, what the fuck is going on? We ain't never have no problems before, now this nigga feeling some way?" I started walking towards Que. "I don't have time for y'all to be losing out on any money because he wanna act like a bitch!" I marched, with Tony and Don following behind me.
"I'm ready for whatever, yo!" Tony lifted up his shirt, exposing a gun.
"Nah, we not even gon' need that. I'ma handle it!"
"And, if he get slick, I'ma handle it my way!" Tony threatened. I didn't even have time to go back and forth with him, so I just nodded my head and put a pep in my step.
"A-yo, what's the issue Que?" I asked, frustrated. "I hear you talking bout we can't come around this way, but I'm trying to figure out who died and made you boss?"

Chuckling, Que rubbed his goatee. "This my block and I say who run through here and who don't. You got a problem with it, then we can definitely handle that!"

"You damn right, I got a problem with that shit! Like I said, I do what the fuck I want. I'm not limited to nothing you niggas say!" I boasted.

"Come thru here and see what can happen, Khalil!" Que walked up on me, my reflexes got the best of me and I punched him in the jaw, causing him to stumble back.

"I told you, nobody bosses me or makes idle threats!" I caught him again and we scuffled until shots rang out. I looked up to see Tony standing to the side, with the gun in his hand. The next thing happened so fast, we barely had time to take cover. Que let off a few shots, in our direction, as we ducked behind a car.

"Nigga you don't boss shit! You can't even be the man in your relationship!" Que spat, as he hopped into his car.

"Oh, this nigga talking slick. I'ma come see him when he's alone. He forgot who he fucking wit'!" I said, to no one in particular, as the 3 of us made our way to the car.

"I told you to let me kill him right then and there!" Tony shouted.

"I wasn't even trying to cause that kind of drama-"

Don chimed-in, cutting me off. "That dude threatened us and you wasn't trying to cause that kind of drama? See, I think you getting soft!"

"Not at all, but I got a family at home that I'm trying to go home to!"

"Yeah, the same family Que said you can't control!" Tony stared in my face, with a hard-grill!

"Fuck you, Tony." Making a turn onto my block, I hopped out of the car before I pulled into my driveway, leaving it at the curb. "I'll be right back." Running up the driveway, I unlocked the door to my house.

"Pilar! Pilar!" I shouted.

"Daddy, I missed you!" Liam came running down the stairs with the biggest grin plastered on his face. Grabbing him up in my arms, I hugged my boy. "Hey, lil man!"

Just then, Pilar appeared on the staircase, bouncing Rue on her chest, trying to soothe her.

"What are you yelling for Kha? What is the emergency?" She asked.

Watching her come down the stairs, I had to shake the feelings of lust because she was glowing and her curls bounced up and down.

"I need to fuck-" I began. Looking down at Liam, I adjusted my language. "I gotta talk to you." I took Rue into my arms. "Hey, daddy's baby. I've missed you, chunk-chunk!"

I rocked her in my arms, more to soothe myself, than to soothe her.

Knowing that a grown-folk's conversation was about to ensue, Liam went back upstairs to his video game, that I had so rudely interrupted.

"Okay, wassup? Cuz you come in here shouting like someone tried to kill you!" She chuckled, as she wiped off the counter.

"You know something I don't, Pilar?" I spoke sternly. "Cuz word on the street is I can't control my wife. So, what the fuck you doing in them streets?"

Pilar turned to me with a shocked look on her face. "What are you talking about, Khalil? I don't know what you hearing but leave it right there and come directly to me!"

"That's what the fuck I'm doing!" I shouted.

Pilar slammed the sponge down on the counter. "No, your ass heard something in the streets and you come accusing me of something instead of calling me and asking me if there's something I need to tell you."

Pilar walked up on me, taking Rue from my arms. "That's exactly why I want a divorce. You letting these streets ruin our marriage." She walked out of the kitchen and I followed. "AND, for the record, I've never been in the streets so why would I start now?"

I sat on the arm of the sofa in disbelief. I came running here because of what Que said, then I let Tony throw it in my face. "What am I thinking? My wife not in them streets!" I said to myself.

Hopping-up, I moved towards Pilar, as she was snapping Rue in her bouncer.

"My bad, lil mama. You right, I'm bugging!" Slapping her on her butt, I headed upstairs to retrieve some more clothes. Entering the room, I looked around. Nothing looked out of place, so I gathered some things and headed towards the door.

"Kha, I'm leaving Friday for Miami. The kids are staying with your mom this time around. I'll be back Tuesday morning."

"Copy, I'll be out there Saturday." I winked, as I left. "Oh! Thanks for telling me."

"Hello? When were you going to tell me that, Kha?" Pilar asked, with her hands on her hips

"This week, but I gotta go. Later, P.!"

"Later." She responded, dryly.

I was relieved that Pilar wasn't messing around, but even more relieved that she was leaving Miami before me, so I had some days to have fun. Que hadn't seen the last of me, but I'll handle that when Pilar was in Miami and the kids in Jersey with my mom.

Avery

Monday morning, I woke up early. I had plans and by leaving Chyanne in the bed sleeping, I knew I had made the right choice or she would blow my cover.

Pulling-up to the front of the building in my black Range Rover, I looked out of the tinted windows, as people started to enter the building.

"Bingo! There you go!" I said, leaning up in my seat. I wanted to get out and approach her, but I knew I couldn't approach her by her job, so I waited until I saw one of her coworkers, to ask what time she would be getting off. I stood outside of the Range, leaning against it, until I saw someone who might answer my question and she did.

"4:30, sometimes 5, why? How you know her?" She snapped.

"She's my home girl. I'm back in town and wanted to surprise her, is that a problem?"

"No, not at all, just checking." She waved and walked away.

"Bitch." I mumbled under my breath, as I got back into my car.

I hung out in the area for the rest of the day until I spotted Pilar coming out of work and rushing to her car. Starting my car up, I followed behind her until she made a stop. I looked around for street signs, since I didn't know the area and didn't want to end up in the wrong hood.

I watched as Pilar exited the house, carrying a baby and a little boy following not too far behind her. "Kids? I don't remember her mentioning kids to me, but someone did, at her job, that day." I thought.

I continued to follow her for a couple of days and learned that her husband hadn't been home. I didn't know if he didn't live with her anymore, but I did know there was no extra car in the driveway. By Wednesday evening Pilar was running later than usual, just as I was about to pull off, I saw her driving up to her house, followed by another car.

"Damn, her husband is here!" I pounded on the steering wheel. "Shit!" Pushing my face up to the window, I saw a guy exit the car and grab up her son. It wasn't her husband though. It was that nigga, Andre.

"Why the fuck is he here? I hope she's not fucking him!" Angry and agitated, I rolled the window down a little as he entered her house. 30 minutes passed and he still hadn't returned to his car. "Oh, so she can't answer my messages, but she can have this nigga in her house."

Pissed off, I started up the car, just as Andre stepped out of the house with Pilar. She gave him a brief hug and he got into his car. My blood boiled as I watched the exchange. I drove off and the car slid a little.

Pulling out my phone, I dialed a number, placing the phone on speaker.

"Hey babe, wassup?"

"That nigga Andre was just with Pilar. I think they're fucking with each other again." I spat.

"You sure about that, Avery?" Chyanne questioned.

"Yeah, I was just over by Pilar house and saw his ass there, hanging out for some time!" I had blown my own cover.

"Over Pilar house? What were you doing over there?"

Thinking fast on my feet, I answered. "Uhh, cuz I was going to approach her about you. I wanted to know what the beef was?" I stuttered.

"Baby, I can handle my own battles, though. So. You need not to worry about that!" Chyanne said. "But Andre was there, huh? What's the address? I'm going to pop up on his ass."

"I'm not going to tell you where she lives, so you can go acting crazy. Your son's father has been ducking you, but he's around his other baby."

"Right! Talking about the streets is too crazy right now, that's why he can't ever take Andrew!" Chyanne sucked her teeth.

"Don't even worry though. I'm headed to you now."

"What you mean 'don't worry'? He is treating my son like shit, while he's parading her son around! I'm not having that"

"Okay, cool, but just relax until I get there." I reasoned.

"Okay, later." Ending the call, I pulled-over to the side of the street and went to my emails. Scrolling, checking for a new email from her, I became frustrated.

"Why the fuck is she not responding? I'm going to step to her tomorrow, I tell you that! She is not going to do this to me!"

Stepping on the gas, I raced to my house to find Chyanne pacing back and forth. "I'm going straight to her house, and if she answers, I'm going to fuck her up." Chyanne shouted in frustration.

"I told you no violence, right? And besides, I'm not giving you the address, Chyanne."

Andre

Bang! Bang!
The banging on my front door startled me.

"Who's banging on my damn door?!" I shouted, walking towards the door.

"Chyanne!" Came the answer.

I unlocked the door and confronted her. "Why the fuck you banging on my damn door like the police, Chy?"

Moving forward, Chyanne slapped me across the face. "I'ma fucking kill you!" She shouted, enraged.

Grabbing a hold of her hands, I restrained her. "Hit me again, Chyanne and I'm going to kill you! What the hell is your problem?"

Struggling to break free of my grasp, she screamed in my face, "Get off of me Andre, you fucking deadbeat!"

Letting her hands go free, I stared at her like she was crazy. "Deadbeat? Bitch did you forget all the money you get a month and how Andrew was just at my house last month? Oh, because I don't want to deal with your grimey-ass I'm a deadbeat? Fuck you!" I spat back.

Chyanne stood there in shock, for a minute, as I went off on her antics. "Oh, that's how you feel?"

"Nah, I should be asking your ass is that how you feel?" I volleyed back.

"Move!" She brushed pass me. "I want to ask you some questions."

"What, Chyanne? Cuz right now, I don't want to talk to you."

"I don't care what you want, cuz guess what I want to know? Why you claim you so busy that you can't see Andrew but your ass be up under Liam little ass?!"

I chuckled, at her. "Oh, that's your problem, because my other baby mama had an emergency and needed me, I'm wrong?"

Tapping her foot, with much attitude, she came back at me. "That's what you call it? If she got a problem her husband clearly can fix it!"

"Bullshit! That's me and her kid and I do for my own damn kids!"

"Right, like you're doing for Andrew, right?"

Walking away from Chyanne, I spat, looking in her direction. "That $5000 I just gave you ain't enough, huh, you fucking gold-digger?!"

"Gold-digger?" Chyanne looked at me, bewildered. "Never that! Money ain't spending time with your kid!"

"You're right! That's why I haven't had Liam here, either. But if your ass had a stable place to stay, then I'd go to your crib. Matter of fact, bring me my son! I can be a better parent than your slut ass!"

"Fuck you!" Chyanne hissed.

Laughing, in her face, I kept it up. "Exactly! I struck a nerve right? All the money I give you and you can't seem to keep an apartment! I'ma take you to court, so my mom could get full custody of my boy."

"Do that and I swear, the cops will know about everything you're involved in!" Chyanne shouted.

"You don't know shit about what I do, so I just may take you up on that challenge, sweetie!" I continued to chuckle. "Now, you're dismissed! I gotta take this call!" Turning and walking off, I answered the phone.

"Wassup?"

"Yo, Chyanne ass is a snake! I can't prove it right now, but I got word that she's been kicking it with some new dude!" Rah spoke into the phone.

"Who's this new dude? And how close do you think they are?" I questioned, rubbing my head. Looking over my shoulder I saw that Chyanne was nowhere in sight.

"Some cat named Avery, if I'm not mistaken."

"Say word?! Get the fuck outta here!" I was truly shocked.

"Yeah, but I'ma hit you, when I get something concrete."

"Say no more... 1"

Ending the call, I was livid. Scrolling through the call log, I dialed her number.

"Hello?" She answered, groggily.

"Get up. I need you to answer some questions for me."

"Right now? I'm napping Andre."

"Yes, Pilar! You said that Avery wasn't the father right?"

"Huh, Andre what are you rambling about?" Pilar asked

"You said that Khalil is your daughter's father and not Avery, right?" I asked anxiously.

"Yes, Andre, she's Khalil's baby, why?"

"Don't worry about it. That's all I wanted to know. Go ahead back to sleep."

"What do you mean, go back to sleep? No, you're going to tell me what's going on Andre!" Pilar shouted into the receiver.

"Relax, baby girl. I heard some shit about him. Pease, tell me you didn't go off of looks that you had a test done."

"No, Andre I didn't get a test done. I know she looks like her dad, okay? You're scaring me and pissing me off, all at the same time!"

"I'm sorry, baby girl. Listen, I'ma holla back at you, in a few, aight?"

She sucked her teeth, annoyed with me. "Fine, Dre."

"Fix your attitude. This is going to benefit you!"

Before Pilar could respond, I heard a noise in my house.

"Hello? Hello?" Pilar shouted.

"Hold on mama, I heard something in my crib."

"Oh, you acting like a punk Dre." Pilar chuckled.

"Never that, but Chyanne was here and I didn't lock the door behind her. Let me call you back, aight?"

"Okay, cool." She ended the call.

I grabbed my gun and walked to the living room with it raised, but no one was there. I noticed that my picture of Pilar and Liam was face down. Raising my eyebrows I knew something was up but I couldn't pin-point it.

I gotta go see this dude Avery. He's starting unnecessary drama that I don't have time for.

Pilar

Stressed wasn't the word! I had my husband blowing me up, wanting to reconcile our differences, but yet he accuses me of cheating. Andre expressing to me that he wanted his family back. Que, who I adored at the moment because he was something fresh and new, but then, that reminds me of the asshole, Avery, who emailed me hate mail one minute and then love mail the next.

Raising my glass to take another sip of the Patron Margarita, I looked over at Lola, "Miami next stop, bitch!"

"Hush yo' drunk-ass up! Sleep is your next stop!" Lola side-eyed me.

"Yeah, P. That's enough drinking. You're going to be too drunk to party." Jewel chastised me, taking the glass from my hand.

"Fine, y'all are party poppers! I'm kid free and soon getting a divorce. Why can't I celebrate?" I whined.

"Cuz you are not leaving Khalil. You just being stubborn." Tasha spat.

"Shut the hell up! You don't know what I'm doing!" I said, rolling my eyes and hopping-off of the bar stool.

"Alright! Y'all gon' cut this damn beef out!" Tamia stated "I don't understand."

"Cuz she always wanna chastise me, like she's my mom!" I whined.

"Oh, please. Your whining is annoying me Pilar. Stop drinking. It doesn't look good on you." Tasha rolled her eyes.

"Fuck you, you didn't have to come if you wanted to act up!" Flipping Tasha the finger, I walked towards the exit. "Our flight is boarding soon."

"C'mon girl, you need to have a seat and relax." Jewel grabbed my hand.

"Pilar, when we get on this flight, your ass needs to take a nap so you can be sobered-up by the time we get to Miami." Lola said catching up to us.

"I guess. I just wanna party, tan and see Que." I winked. Lola and Jewel knew I planned on seeing Que but my sisters had no idea. I wanted to keep it a secret and act as if I had just run into him.

"Oh, I bet your freaks ass do!" Lola laughed.

As soon as we boarded the flight, the liquor took over and I was out cold, sprawled across Tamia and Jewel.

"Welcome to Miami!" The Captain announced.

"Get your ass up!" Tamia slapped my thigh.

"Okay, okay! I'm up!" I stretched, feeling rejuvenated. That nap was just what I needed.

"Let's go so we can get some of this sun!" Lola squealed, grabbing her bag.

"Well, someone is excited!" I chuckled "Where's Jewel?"

"In the bathroom. I think her man is mad." Lola said. "Glad I don't have no man issues."

"Ha, cute! Let me go check on her." We walked towards the restroom, just as Jewel was walking out. "What's up?"

"Nothing, I forgot to tell my boo I was boarding the plane. He was worried." Jewel shrugged and walked to retrieve her bag.

Looking at her walk away, I could tell something was bothering her, but I was going to wait for her to explain.

"Let's go!" Tasha shouted, snapping me out of my daydream. Raising my hand to let her know I was coming I pulled out my phone to call Ms. Grace, Khalil's mom, to check in on the kids. After I spoke to the kids I ended the call and my phone began to ring.

Ring! Ring!

"Hello?"

"Hey, baby girl, you in Miami already?" Andre asked.

"Yeah, I'm here. Wassup?"

"Oh, when you get back in the city, hit my line. I gotta holla at you, aight?" Dre spoke.

"Okay, but if it's urgent, you can tell me now, Dre. If it's about Liam, I'll have it arranged so you can have him!" I said out of concern.

"Nah, I'm good. Let him hang with his sister. I'll have him next week. It ain't urgent. Don't stress. Go enjoy you some Pilar time." Andre chuckled.

"Why you laughing?"

"Just thinking about when your ass was here going crazy. Now you got a peace of mind, so enjoy it!" Dre said.

"Ok, fine." I laughed it off. "I'ma holla, time to go enjoy some drinks." I squealed.

"Do ya thang, girl... 1!"

Ending the call, I dropped my bags on the floor and stepped out of my shoes. I looked for the girls. I didn't hear them. The beach house Que rented was very relaxing, yet spacious.

"Shots! Shots! Shots!" Tasha shouted. "Throw that shit back Mia!"

I could hear someone banging on the table, as I came down the stairs.

"Shit! That tequila is strong! Yuck!" Tasha frowned, pouring another round of shots. I laughed at these crazy girls.

"Your turn, Lola." Tamia slid the glasses in her direction.

"I'm ready." Lola threw back the 2 shots. "Let's go!" Lola jumped off the stool heading for the stereo system. Shaking my head, I was happy that I had decided to come to Miami.

"Okay, Jewel, it's your turn!" I shouted from behind them.

"I don't like tequila, but for you, baby, I'll do it," Jewel pouted.

"Good!" I grabbed the bottle of tequila, poured her shots and handed them to her. Tasha grabbed the other two glasses and drank the shots.

"That's what I'm talking about! Pilar, I don't know if you want anything else to drink, right now, or you wanna wait until later?" Tamia asked.

"I want a pre-game! Don't play me! Pour up my shots!"

"Well, alright!" Jewel yelled.

Pre-gaming for another hour before we got ready to hit the pool party, we were all a little tipsy.

Deciding on my baby pink 2-piece cheeky bikini and jean shorts, I finished off my look with Ray-Ban sunglasses and FENTY flip flops. Throwing my hair in a messy bun, I applied a touch of pink lip gloss and grabbed my wallet.

"Y'all heifers better be ready!" I yelled, walking into the living room.

"Yeah, chick, we ready. You the one who took forever to throw on nothing!" Lola scrunched up her nose.

"Oh, I know you not talking. Besides, we're going to a pool party, why in the hell would I be dressed?" I said, placing my hands on my hips.
"Girl, please, your ass would be half naked no matter where we were going." Jewel laughed, tapping my arm.

"So, I don't like clothes. It's hot. Don't focus on me, mama, cuz I'ma make it do what it do!" I laughed.

"I'm sure your fast ass is!" Lola slapped a high five with me.

"Let's go!" Tasha yelled.

"This heifer getting on my nerves!" I rolled my eyes.

"Mine too!" Jewel and Lola agreed in unison.

Stepping out of the house, I saw the S-Class Mercedes that Que left for me to drive. Smiling on the inside, I took out my phone and shot him a text.

Pilar- I'm loving the house and car, thanks hunny...

As I placed my phone in the car, it beeped.

Que-You're welcome. I can't wait to get you in my arms I miss ya ass :)

A huge smile came across my face.

"Hello?!" Lola waved her arms in my face.

"Let's go get something to eat before we get to the party." she suggested.

"Aight. Y'all know what y'all want?"

"Fat Tuesday's!" Jewel blurted-out.

"Sounds like a plan!" I started-up the car and we were off to enjoy our first night.

Eating, talking and dancing was what our night involved, until my phone stopped me short.

"Hello?" I asked, irritated.

"So, you wasn't going to call me and let me know you got there safe Pilar?"

"My bad, I got here and started partying. What, I can't enjoy myself?" I sucked my teeth.

"Yeah, you can enjoy yourself and you better not be out there wilding, Pilar."

"Or what? We are separated Khalil, did you forget?"

"You still carry my last name, wearing my ring, your ass still my fucking wife, then, so don't get fucked up!" Khalil shouted into the phone.

"Fine, Kha, I'm not trying to argue. I'm out here, so let me enjoy this, damn!" I said in frustration.

"Aight, but remember what I said. I'ma holla. I love you."

Looking at the phone, rolling my eyes, I ended the call, annoyed. "Love you too, Kha."

"Love you too, Kha." Lola mimicked.

"Shut up and don't repeat that, Lola."

She laughed. "I'm not. Your secret is safe with me." Lola made the sign of the cross.
"Let's go, silly!" We grabbed our drinks and headed to the pool party.

"Twerk for me!" Jewel shouted, as I twerked to the music. Throwing up one hand and holding my drink in the next, we partied until I felt someone grab my waist.

"So, this is what you doing, huh?" Hearing him, made chills go down my spine. Turning to face him I tried to hide my blushing face.

"Hey, you!" I reached-up to give him a hug.

"Hey, me? That's how you doing it? I want more than that." Que leaned in to my ear

"You shouldn't be dancing like that, unless you're on me."

I smirked. "Is that right"

"Hell yeah! What you mean?" Que said, pulling me in close.

"Babe, my sisters don't know about us." Looking around, I spotted Tasha glaring at me. "I'm going to text you, later, so we can meet up."

"Fuck you mean so we can meet up? You staying in my beach house! I can come by there, if I want to!" Que spat.

"Quinn you know how my sisters are!" I reached to touch him. He snatched his arm back.

"You always on some shit, Pilar! This is why I stay the fuck away from your sometimey ass!" He hissed, walking off.

"Quinn, hello? You're not going to walk away from me with no attitude!" I demanded.

"Go keep partying, Pilar I'ma holla at you!" Waving me off, Que then hopped in a car and drove off.

"Stupid ass." I mumbled, catching my breath after running after Que.

"What was that about?" Tasha asked, walking up on me.

"Nothing, don't worry about it." I waved her off.

"You fucking him, Pilar?" Tasha blatantly asked.

"Why are you worried about that Tasha?" I asked.

"Because he obviously going hard, so something is up!" Tasha quipped.

"Well, don't worry about what I do. I'm grown."

"Yeah, you fucking him. Well, I hope you not divorcing Khalil because you running behind that street dude!" Tasha spat.

"Oh, so you know what I'm doing with my life, huh? Do you really know everything or you're just being the over protective sister that you have always been?" I showed her my palm. "Don't even answer because I don't care. I'm going back to the party!" Walking away from Tasha, I went to sit on the side and rummage through my phone, until I was frustrated and ready to leave.

"Hey girlie, you okay?" Jewel tapped my shoulder.

"Yeah, I'm good. Let me know when y'all ready to leave. I'm finished drinking for the day."

"If you ready, we can go, now. I'll tell the girls." Jewel started to walk off.

"Nah, don't do that, I'll wait." Jewel nodded her head and walked away.

A few hours later, the girls were sprawled out on their beds, drunk and I was sitting on my bedroom balcony alone, dialing Que's number, repeatedly, to no avail.

Ring! Ring! My phone vibrated in my hand scaring me.

"Hello?" I answered agitated.

"Cut all that noise out. What are you doing?"

"Minding my damn business, not worried about you!" I rolled my eyes, as though he could see me.

"Be ready in 10 minutes."

"I'm not going anywhere with you. As a matter of fact, I'm going to tell the girls to pack up, in the morning and we can book a room."

"Yeah, aight, whatever! Be ready, Pilar!" He hung up the phone in my ear. I looked at the phone then placed it on the table. Grabbing a bottle of wine, I filled-up a glass and sipped it. Letting the night breeze blow through my hair, I continued to sit and ignore Que's request.

"I don't know who these guys think they are, talking to me anyway and expect me to be quiet." I sighed. "I don't know why I started dating in the first place. I should have never dated." Shaking my head from side to side, I started to feel the Taylor Port.

Ring! Ring!

"Yes!"

"Get out here, Pilar. Don't make me come in there to get you!" Que barked.

"You're not my daddy and I don't have to listen to your ass!" I barked back.

"Pilar, Pilar! Get out here, now!"

"Bye, Que. I want to be left alone!" I ended the call before he could respond. I took a hefty gulp of what was left in the glass and laid my head back on the chair. Closing my eyes, I started to feel the effects of the wine.

"Ahh." I sighed. Dozing off in less than 5 minutes, I was awakened by a tap on my leg, almost making me jump out of my skin.

"Shit!"

"Didn't I tell you to bring your ass downstairs, Pilar?" Que questioned aggressively.

"I don't care what you say, Que-" Before I could finish, Que was kneeled down cocking my legs open. Picking me up, Que held me up against the ledge of the balcony. Kissing me and undoing my bikini top, I moaned in ecstasy.

"Um, Que, stop!"

Ignoring me, he made his way to my breast, as they spilled out of my top. Taking my left nipple into his mouth and massaging my right, I couldn't fight it. Throwing my head back and holding onto the ledge, for balance, I moaned. Que teased me and then we made our way to the bedroom. Trying to hold in my moans with the pillow, I scratched at Que and bit on his collarbone. For the next hour, we pleased each other. I climaxed several times, until finally, we climaxed together.

"Kh, Que, umm I'll be right back." I jumped-up from the bed, hoping he didn't hear me slip up. Once I was in the bathroom, I turned on the shower and thought out loud. "Fuck, what was I thinking, almost calling him Khalil. I gotta stop this shit. I've started something and set off a beast in Que." I hopped in the shower, thinking,"This dude gets turned on by my aggressiveness. I'm not about this life and nope, I don't want to do this anymore."

Knock! Knock!

The soap slipped out of my hand, as I was startled from my thoughts.

"Yeah?"

"So, you wanna shower alone?" Que spoke through the closed door.

"Umm, I didn't think you was coming. Hold on." I stepped out of the shower and a cool breeze hit me, causing me to catch a chill. "I'm almost finished and I'm exhausted Quinn." I said, as I opened the door.

"Okay, I'll leave before your girls get up. You don't have to kick me out my shit!"

I rolled my eyes, as we stepped into the shower. This possessive shit was annoying me. "I didn't say that, but whatever, Que". Turning my back towards him, I stood under the water, letting it flow over me.

Spinning me around, Que pinned me up against the shower door, leaning in to my ear, "Don't ever compare me to that corny-ass husband of yours." He moved his hand down my chest taking my breast into his hand. "You gon' make it up to me"? He questioned.

Pushing him off of me, gently, I responded. "No, I'm not. It was an honest mistake. Get off of me, Quinn, you're starting to make me mad!" Pushing pass him I opened the shower door and exited the shower.

"Where are you going, Pilar? Don't do that, you're going to piss me off!" Que demanded.

"I don't care anymore, Quinn. I should have never come here. I should have left the ticket in your house!" Grabbing the towel, I wrapped my body and exited the bathroom. Once I was in the room, I quickly threw on my night shirt and boy shorts. I was applying lotion to my legs, when Que stepped out of the bathroom, looking in my direction. "So, you just gon' walk away while I'm talking to you?"

"Quinn, I just said I'm fucking tired. I don't want to fight because that's not what I came here for, but guess what you are starting to act like my corny ass husband." I quoted, grabbing the comforter and pulling it back. "Now, I don't care if you want your little house back, cool. I have no problem staying in a hotel, but I will not keep going back and forth with you."

"That's how you feel, Pilar?" Que stopped getting dressed and stared at me.

"Apparently, I said it, right?" I snapped, throwing my feet up on the bed.

"You must be going through PMS or something, so I'ma leave you alone tonight, but I'ma call you tomorrow, so answer."

"Whatever." Rolling my eyes, I pulled the cover over my head and fell back on the bed.

The next day I slept until 12pm, while the girls were out back sunbathing and gossiping.

"Well, good afternoon Princess." Tamia snickered when I stepped-off the staircase.

"Shut up, silly!"

"I'm saying, he put it down like that?" Lola laughed.

"Shut up, I damn near drank the whole Taylor Port!" I threw a towel at her.

"Baby girl, come here, let me talk to you!" Tasha yelled over the music. Looking at Tamia and Lola, I rolled my eyes, mumbling, "Not today".

I picked-up a cup of ice tea and grabbed a strawberry. "Yeah, wassup?" I asked, flopping down in the chair.

"Look, I know you seeing Que. I don't care. You're grown, but I want you to be careful. I know you're only doing this because you are mad at Khalil, but in the end, I don't want you to have any regrets." Tasha chastised, the way she does.

"I know what I'm doing." I hopped up, not in the mood for a lecture.

"Pilar, we are not finished here." Tasha said.

"Listen sis I know-" Tamia spoke, cutting me off.

"Wrong, you don't know, Pilar. You just giving-in to these dudes. I don't care if you want to chea,t but you playing with fire, cheating with a dude that has beef with your husband and your sons father!" Tamia pointed out. "Listen, we love you and we are not being hard on you, but I don't want you to slip up."

Sitting back down in the chair, I decided to let what they said marinate. "Okay. Y'all are right, yes, I'm hurting because my husband is cheating on me and yes I'm messing with a dude that he doesn't like, but nobody lectures Khalil, so why do I have to get lectured?"

"Cuz that nigga ain't my business, you are!" Tasha pointed at me.

"Okay. I hear y'all, I'll be careful." I stood up. "Can I be excused? I want to go to the beach, then KOD, today."

"Go ahead. Just think about what we are saying, Pilar." Tamia said, touching my arm.

"Yes, Ms. Stubborn." Tasha agreed.

"I am." I smiled and walked off. I headed to the bedroom to find which bikini I was wearing tonight.

"Sexy or classy, hmm?" I held up the bikinis to my chest, modeling which look I would decide on. Coming to a decision, I figured I'd wear my turquoise high cut bikini with my white mesh cover-up dress.

"Why not, I'm in Miami. I want to show off a bit."

Laying-out my outfit for the club tonight and applying my makeup, I got dressed.

"Ladies, lets go to the beach, now." I whined

"Okay, cool, mama. Let me go get dressed." Lola hopped out of the pool and grabbed her towel.

Waiting on them to get dressed I pulled out my phone to call my babies and catch up with Khalil, but had no luck reaching him.

"I hope I don't run into him on this trip." I spoke to myself.

"We are all ready!" Jewel stated.

Looking at all my girls, I was pleased with all of their tastes. On the beach, we ordered our drinks and found a spot with enough sun for tanning.

With the music blasting and gossiping about things at home, we were having a great time, together.

"Can I get a Refill?" I shouted over to Tamia. "Pour it up, pour it up!" I held up my glass, while shaking my ass. My phone started ringing. Not looking at the caller, I answered.

"Hello?!" I shouted over the music.

"What the fuck you got on, Pilar? You think you cute huh?"

Looking around, I couldn't spot where he was, but the music on his end told me he wasn't far away.

"I have on a bikini. I'm at the beach! This is what you wear to the beach." I spat.

"Take that shit off, right now!"

"I will not!" I removed the phone from my ear. I couldn't make-out what he was saying, but I heard him shouting. Ending the call, I chuckled and turned my attention back to my girls.

Bending over to reach for my beach bag, I was snatched-up. "You really think I'm playing with you, Pilar! I said to go take that shit off!" Khalil yelled.

"Get off of me, Kha. I'm on damn vacation!" Pulling my arm away from him, he grabbed my arm again and pulled me in close. "I said take that string the fuck off! You wanna come out here acting like a hoe? I will embarrass you, Pilar!"

Slapping him with my free hand, I spazzed on him. "Don't ever call me out of my name!"

"Khalil get off of her! Damn, she's on the fucking beach!" Tamia shouted.

"I don't care where the fuck she is! Showing that much ass is unacceptable! Now, let's go!" He pulled me up off of the beach, with my girls following behind us. Those were my ride or dies, for sure.

Once we were in Khalil's room I went in the bathroom and slapped him again.

"Really? You going to embarrass me, like that?"

"Take it off, Pilar. Take it off!" Khalil grabbed at my bikini, getting a hold of the string under my boob and stretching it. After fighting for the next few minutes, Khalil finally left the bathroom.

"I hope it was worth it, all them scratches on your face!" Tasha laughed.

He held the bikini top up. "It was well worth it!" He said, winking and exiting the room.

"Pilar, what the fuck?" Tasha yelled through the door.

"I don't know and I don't care." I opened the door, wearing a maxi dress from my beach bag. "I'm always prepared. Now, I need to go to this club tonight, cuz he done blew my whole day!" I said rolling my eyes "Fucking asshole!"

"Strip clubs and dollar bills. I still got my money. Patron shots can I get a refill?"

Blasted from the DJ booth, as I sang along with Rhianna holding-up my filled shot glass. My girls and I were at KOD tonight, VIP with no drama and no guys.

"Pop that thang!" Tamia shouted, over the music while Jewel and Lola danced along to the music.

"Girl, come with me to the bathroom." Jewel pushed past Lola, grabbing my arm.

"Okay, hold on let me put this glass down." Following behind Jewel, I spotted Khalil across from us. Looking more closely, I saw a thick chick leaning over, whispering in his ear. The smirk that was plastered on his face told me she was up to no good and he was feeding into it.

"How bad do you have to go Jewel?"

"Bad, why wassup?"

"Nothing, let's hurry up! Afterward, I'ma need you to roll with me."

"Okay, let me empty my bladder first." Jewel rushed into the stall, while I looked myself over in the mirror. Fixing my boobs and smoothing down the side of my midi dress I shouted, "C'mon, Jewel! Damn, what you letting out a river in there, girl?" Applying my lipstick and brushing down my hair, swooping one side behind my ear, I was ready to pay my husband a visit.

"I'm all set." Jewel grabbed the paper towel.

"Are you good?"

"I'm great, but I see Khalil has some company and I plan on squashing that!" Walking out of the bathroom, taking the lead, Jewel followed right behind.

"Cool, say no more."

Looking in his direction again, I saw him leaning up on the wall and yet again, she was whispering in his ear, but what disgusted me was her hand was down his shorts.

"Fuck this bitch think she doing?" I mumbled. Yeah, I said I wanted a divorce and yes, I was currently fucking Quinn, it was because of shit like this that had me choosing to go down that road. I stepped up on her but it wasn't her fault, so I reached over her and slapped the side of Khalil's head. Catching him off guard, he stumbled and looked surprised.

"P, what the fuck, yo?" He asked.

"What the fuck, Kha? This is exactly why I'm filing for divorce when I get back to the city." I shouted, slapping him again.

"You gon' stop putting your hands on me!" Khalil screamed, as he regained his balance, but I just continued to hit him until I was pulled away by Jewel. By the time I looked around, the girl was nowhere to be found.

"She's lucky, cuz I swear that's the same chick from before."

"C'mon, girl, just calm down." Jewel said pulling me away. Pissed off, I yanked away from Jewel.

"I'm outta here! I'm over repeating this shit and I'll meet y'all at the house. I just need to be alone!" I said walking off.

"Pilar, don't leave me. I'm coming with you." Jewel followed but I put my hand up to stop her.

"Nah, Jewel, I just want to be alone. Can you respect that, please?" I asked.

"Fine, call me."

Tossing Jewel the keys to the house, I walked away.

I found myself repeating the same thing over and over. I was drained.

Knock! Knock!

"Hey, what you doing here?"

"Are you busy?" I asked, leaning against the door.

"Nah, nah, come in." Que said, moving out of the way. "I'm just surprised you came here, after I've been calling you all day."

"Yeah, I know." I said, sitting down on the couch. "I don't know if I'm here because I'm mad or because I want to be with you, but I just needed to get out of that club."

"What are you mad about?" Que asked going into the kitchen.

"Just how everything is going. You-"

Que's phone started ringing, stopping me midsentence.

"I can ignore that call. I'm with you, so talk to me." Que said pouring two glasses of wine.

"I don't want anything to drink. I'm good." Holding up my hand to stop him.

Ring! Ring!

Que's phone began to ring again, with a text.

"Can you pass me that, please?" He asked.

Before taking the phone over to him, I noticed the message read:

-Khalil isn't feeling me right now his wife came here fighting him and shit -Sasha

Twisting my nose up, in disgust, I slammed his phone into his chest and folded my arms across my chest.

"What's your problem? You're starting to act bipolar, Pilar." Que said unlocking his phone and replying to the message.

"So, you're just going to respond to that message like I'm not right here?" I spat.

"Calm down, this is work. You acting jealous now?" He looked down at his phone and sent another message.

"Work? Oh, so setting Sasha up with Khalil was your job, Quinn?" I walked up on Que. "I can't believe you!" I chuckled. "But, I can't even be mad, cuz he's a grown man and should have turned her down. But, you set it up. Why Que, why?" I questioned.

"Listen, I didn't set-"

"Bullshit, don't lie to me, why?"

"I didn't think he was going to fall for it, but he did, so I went along with pursuing you, Pilar. It wasn't all that bad. We reconnected." Que stated.

I mushed his chest, wanting to really punch him. "Fuck you! What we had is dead. I'll be back to bring you your keys and I'm going home." Picking up my clutch to leave, Que jumped in front of me. "Where are you going?"

"Like I just said I'm leaving. No love lost. My husband is at fault, but I never expected you to stoop this low." Brushing pass Que, I left.

I shut off my phone and entered the house. The girls were all there with worried looks on their faces.

"Where have you been?" Tasha asked

"Handling some business. I'm going to book us a room and we can just leave from the hotel tomorrow."

"A room, why?" Lola asked.

"This is Que's house and I just cut him off because the chick, Sasha, well he set her up with distracting Khalil so he could get close to me." I looked away as my voice cracked from the hurt. "And, furthermore, I want nothing else to do with him."

"You don't have to explain. Let's pack, girls." Tasha said

Once in the room, I silently cried and packed my bags. The rest of the night I thought of all the things I needed to do differently and that was to stop partying, drinking and looking for love. Instead I needed to put my focus and energy on me and my kids.

Back In NYC...

"It feels good to be home." I mouthed, as I went to the door to get my babies.

"Mommy! Mommy!" Liam yelled, running into my open arms. Hearing Rue's coo, I knew this is where I needed to be.

Khalil

"Hello? Hello?" I answered irritated.

"Khalil, listen, I don't want you coming home. I want you to pack your shit and go stay with that Sasha bitch!" Pilar shouted into the phone.

"Kill all that noise! I'm not staying with no bitch! I'm coming home and we are going to work this shit out!" Agitated, I shouted into the phone.

"No, I'm through with working out anything with you! How could you continue to see that girl, after I caught you and her, before?" Pilar's voice cracked when she spoke. "I can't believe I even married your dog ass!"

"Pilar, hear me out. I want to see you face to face. If you trying to leave me be, a woman and say it to my face!" I shouted.

"Oh, I definitely will, with no problem!" She spat, ending the call.

Finding out that Que had set Sasha up to get with me, had me livid.

"Fucking coward-ass nigga! All cuz he wanted my wife." Shaking my head from side to side, I thought, "Damn! So, that means Pilar had to fuck him, at least once!"

"Fuck!" I spoke out loud, pulling up to the airport.

Ring! Ring!

Looking down at my ringing phone the number was restricted so I sent it to voicemail only to receive another one.

"Hello?!" I answered, annoyed.

"Hello, can I speak to Khalil?" The caller spoke calmly. The voice sounded familiar but I couldn't put a name to it.

"Speaking!"

"You need to get a DNA test for your daughter. I have proof that Pilar slept around and it may be a chance the baby belongs to Avery." The voice said.

Looking at the phone, with my face screwed-up, the call ended and I had no trace of who was on the other end.

"What the fuck is going on?" I looked up and realized that it was boarding time for my plane and I didn't have a chance to call Pilar.

"I swear on everything, this bitch is dead, when I get to New York." I mumbled.

"I told you to leave her alone from the jump." Don spoke. "But, noooo, you wanna listen to Tony young ass."

"Nah, it ain't even that bitch, Sasha, it's my wife." I clinched my hands together and sat down. With my blood boiling and a 3 hour flight ahead of me, I became angrier by the minute.

Once we were off of the flight, I gave my boys dap and headed straight for my house.

"Don't do nothing stupid, Kha. Be rational, a'ight?!" Don yelled.

"Fuck that. I'ma holla, tho!" I hopped in my car and hit a U-turn.

Pulling up to the house, I didn't even park in the garage. I left the car outside and bum rushed the front door. As I fumbled with the key, the door swung open and Carol was on the other end

"Pilar! Pilar!" I yelled, as I brushed pass Carol.

"Well, hello to you too, Khalil!" Carol said sarcastically, as I barged in, ignoring her.

"Pilar!" I continued to yell, taking the stairs in twos. Pilar popped her head out of Rue's nursery.

"Shhh, before you wake her up, Kha. Damn!"

"Pilar, get out here, now!" I demanded.

"Okay." She walked out of the room. "What are you coming in-"

I put my hands around her neck and began choking her. Pilar reflexes kicked in and she clawed at my face, but I continued to squeeze her neck until I saw her face becoming pale.

"I can't fucking believe your hoe ass! You fucked that nigga! You fucked him Pilar?!"

Gasping for air, Pilar fell to the floor, holding her neck. I walked up on her, as she backed up until she hit the wall and couldn't go anywhere.

"Did you fuck him, Pilar? Did you?!" I shouted, bending down in her face. Pilar held her neck as the tears fell from her eyes, which upset me even more. I picked Pilar up, slamming her into the wall. Pilar started fighting back, slapping and kicking.

"Get off of me, you're crazy!" She cried, trying to scream but her voice was hoarse.

"Khalil, get off of my daughter! Now!" Carol shouted. "I will kill you, Khalil! Get the fuck off of her right now and leave!"

Turning to face Carol, I saw the gun in her hand and released Pilar. Looking down at Pilar, she lay on the floor trying to catch her breath.

"Answer me, Pilar! Did you fuck Avery?"

The look on her face told me the answer but I wanted to hear it from her mouth.

"I'm going to ask you one more time!" I kneeled down on the floor again. She looked in my eyes and went to grab my hand. I pushed her hand off of me.

"Fucking bitch!" I spat, taking off the wedding band and throwing it in her face. "You can have that divorce you want!"

"Kha, Kha!" Pilar tried to speak.

"Nah, don't talk now. Is Rue my daughter, Pilar?" She looked at me and nodded her head 'yes'.

"Fuck you!" I spat. I didn't believe a word of it.

I walked past Carol. "I'm sorry." I mouthed and held my head down as I left the house.

Pissed, annoyed and hurt, I drove around for hours looking for Avery. I needed answers and I needed them now!!!

Avery

Chyanne had come forward with information about Pilar but I was unable to reach her. I watched her house and job for days and came up empty.

"A baby, a fucking baby." I mumbled. "How did I not catch that when I was at her job and they asked about her baby?" Shaking my head back and forth, I told myself, "I'm going to her house. I don't care who's there!"

Jumping up from the chair, I ran out of the door. Hopping into my car, I headed straight to her house.

On arrival, looking around, I saw two cars out front, but I wasn't sure if one belonged to her husband. Apprehensive, I walked to the house and knocked on the door. After two knocks, I was ready to walk away when I heard someone come to the door.

"Who is it?"

"Avery."

"Who?" Carol asked.

I heard the locks unlock. "Can I help you?"

Looking in her face, I could see the resemblance she and Pilar shared.

"Uhh, yeah, umm, I know Pilar. Can I speak to her, please?" I stuttered.

"Pilar, there is a young man here for you!" Carol yelled. "Come in."

Stepping inside, I noticed the little boy from before, playing with his toys. Hearing footsteps, I looked up and saw Pilar. She had this shocked look on her face but what really caught my attention was the redness in her eyes.

"What are you doing here, you fucking bastard? Get the fuck out of my house!" Pilar yelled. "Get out!"

"Pilar, listen, I came here in peace-"

"Peace? Peace? No, you started this shit, you!" Pilar pointed at me, yelling. She stopped when she noticed her son's face.

"What are you talking about Pilar? Is there someplace we can talk?" I asked, pleading. I was lost and didn't know what she was referring to. I followed behind her, as she walked away.

"Pilar, please stop and talk to me, what happened?"

Pilar stopped at the top of the stairs. "I know you're the reason my husband found out about our one night stand. I don't care. I hope you're happy!"

"What are you talking about?" I walked up on her, stopping her in her stride and looked in her pale face. Reaching up to touch her cheek, she jerked back from me. "Baby face, what happened to you?" I then noticed the marks on her neck.

"Just leave me alone. I ignored you and you told my husband. You wanted pay back and you got it, Avery. Are you fucking happy?!" Pilar cried. "I give up. I just can't do any more of this! I'm so tired!" Pilar flopped on the bed and sobbed.

"Pilar, I didn't say anything to your husband. I was coming to confront you about this baby." I said reaching for her arm

"Just go. Don't worry about my baby, Avery! Just don't!" She raised her voice and stared at me.

"Pilar, I want to know if she's mine. I have that right to know!" I chastised.

"She's not, so that's it!" Pilar yelled. "Just get out!" She pointed towards the door.

"Either you are willingly going to give me a DNA or I'm going to have to go to your husband!" I demanded. I knew that was a low blow but I had to be stern with Pilar.

"Right, like you haven't already? I don't care!" Pilar cried, again. "She's not yours, leave it at that!" She wiped her face and I wanted to console her, but I needed her to know I was serious. Shaking my head, I looked at Pilar, as she cried and walked down the stairs.

"So, you're the other guy, huh?"

"Yes, ma'am, I am." I spoke solemnly.

"Well, I'm her mother, Carol and I hope that this shit gets resolved and fast. Pilar slipped up, but y'all will not gang up on my daughter!" Carol warned.

I didn't want to argue with her, so I shook my head and left.

Pulling out my phone, I called Chyanne.

"So, you told Pilar's husband about the possibilities or you told one of your blabber mouth friends, Erika or Brittany?" I questioned.

"First off, you will not question me like I'm your child. Pilar fucked-up and as always, y'all want to have her back!" Chyanne barked.

"Y'all? What you mean y'all? Chyanne, if you had anything to do with her husband finding out, it's going to cause issues between us!" I shouted.

"Oh, now it's going to be issues between us?" She snickered. "Spare me Avery!"

"You had no right! You had no right!" I yelled.

"Whatever, you're a bitch ass nigga, sprung on Pilar!" Chyanne shouted and hung-up, in my ear.

Pacing back and forth I didn't know what the next move was, but I did know I needed proof that I wasn't the father.

Andre

"Hello, hello, hello!" I shouted into the phone.

"Andre, I need you!" Pilar frantically shouted into the phone.

"What happened, baby girl? Is everything ok?" I asked, concerned.

"No, I'm not ok, Andre. I'm confused and hurt. I want my husband to come home, but he's not." She cried into the phone.

"Baby girl, relax, I'm coming over!" I jumped up out of the bed.

"I don't know if that's a good idea, Andre. I just want you to stay on the phone with me, please." She pleaded.

"Pilar, I think I should make sure that you and the kids are safe, okay?"

"My mom is here." she solemnly replied

"Okay then, I'll stay on the line until you're ready to go to bed." I said, disappointed.

"Thank you."

"So vent, tell me what's going on."

"He knows, he knows I slept with Avery. He knows about all of it and I don't know who told him. Avery knows about Rue." She sighed. "He came to my house and demanded a DNA test and on top of that, Khalil is asking for one!" She sniffed. "My life is just fucked up all because I decided to have one night of fun, one fucking night!" Pilar shouted in frustration.

"Pilar it's going to be okay, relax. I'm sure it's not as deep as you're making it." I reassured her.

"What? Not that deep, Andre! I have hand marks on my neck and I'm hoarse from Khalil choking me! My husband nearly killed me and you're talking about it's not that deep?" Pilar shouted through sobs.

"Pilar, he did what?!" I heard everything she said but I was stuck on the fact that he put his hands on her. "Pilar where were the kids, where was my son?" I asked pissed.

"He, he was, he was here, Andre" Pilar stuttered as her voice got lower.

"I'm going to kill him! My son saw this happen? Did he?" I questioned her.

"No, Dre, he was with my mom." Pilar spoke, almost in a whisper.

"Don't lie to me. Now is not the time to lie to me, baby girl!"

"He didn't." Pilar cried. "I promise he didn't. I didn't call to make things worse, Andre, please!" Pilar pleaded on the other end.

The phone then went silent as I thought about what I was going to do.

"Pilar, have you seen Chyanne?!" I asked.

"No I haven't, why?" Pilar questioned.

"I think she has something to do with Khalil finding out about Rue and you sleeping with Avery." I responded.

"But how would she know Avery? It's not making any sense to me, Andre."

"That I don't know, but last week when you opened up about it over the phone, I think she was still here."

"What?" Pilar got quiet. "So what you're saying is that she was at your house when I was talking to you Andre?!" Pilar yelled.

"Yes, that's what I'm saying. I told you, she was here and I hadn't heard her leave. That's when you teased me about being a punk!"

"I gotta go, Andre." Pilar said and the phone line went dead.

Thinking on my toes, I headed straight to Chyanne's house. Using the spare key, I unlocked the door and was blown away.

Chyanne

"What the fuck are you doing here?" I shouted, jumping up from Avery.

"What the fuck you mean, what am I doing here? What the fuck is he doing here, Chyanne?" Andre shouted heading towards the bed.

"This is my house and you are not my man! I think I'm entitled to fuck who I want!" I shouted back, grabbing my robe and covering my bare body.

"You're a low down dirty bitch!" Andre chuckled. "You are the most conniving, grimiest bitch I know!"

"Screw you! I'm conniving? You fucked me, had a baby and then fucked my friend and did the same thing!" I yelled at him, in frustration.

"Yea and I learned my lesson, but you-" He paused and shook his head. "You will do whatever it is to make Pilar's life a living hell!"

Then, looking at Avery, accusingly, "And, you have some nerve requesting a DNA test on her daughter!"

"That baby can very well be my child!" Avery yelled.

Andre shook his head and looked at me with disgust.

"Stay the fuck away from Pilar, the both of you or I will have her come whoop yo ass again, Chyanne!" He walked-up close on me. "And if you continue to fuck this clown ass nigga I'm going to take my son away from you!"

"You can't do that Andre! You will never win! I wish you would try to take my baby away from me!" I yelled.

"Fuck you and try me, bitch!" Andre knocked all of the stuff off my dresser and left out, slamming the door behind him.

"Why does he have a key?" Avery shouted, raising his hands in the air.

"I forgot he had it. Why did you approach Pilar without the papers for a DNA?" I questioned.

"Because I didn't want to." Avery picked up his clothes and started getting dressed.

"Well, she is getting everything she deserves. She stole my man!" I spat.

"Whatever, yo, I'm out!" Avery brushed pass me and left.

Sighing, I didn't know if I had gone too far or if this was exactly what Miss Pilar needed.

"Fuck her! Avery wants a DNA test and in order to get him back on my side, I'll just set that up for him." I mumbled to myself, as I picked up everything off the floor.

"I know Robert said stay away from her, but how could I, when the opportunity presented itself?" A smile crept across my face. "I got the perfect idea".

Khalil

No luck in finding Avery. I went to the hotel where he was staying and waited for hours, after knocking on the door, but he never showed up. I couldn't believe my wife had cheated on me and now I'm here second guessing the paternity of Rue. Pulling out my phone I looked over pictures of me and Rue analyzing our facial features.

"She gotta be mine, she has my freckles and my chinky eyes." Shaking my head and pulling the phone closer, I took a good look. "I saw that dude and she looks nothing like him. Yeah, that's my baby girl, that's my chunk chunk." I sighed, falling back into the seat.

"This shit ain't right! My wife, my fucking wife had sex with this dude." I banged my fists on the steering wheel. "I know I fucked up, but damn, I didn't think she was serious about fucking around." I sat in the car a little bit longer trying to put the pieces together. I tried to think of when she met him and if the times matched. I wanted so badly to call her and find out the truth, but I also knew she wouldn't answer because I had put my hands on her.

"Shit, I was mad and she only made it worse by playing stupid, fuck!"

Starting up the car, I just drove. I drove until I ended up at my mother's house.

"Hey, Ma." Walking in and kissing her cheek.

"Hey, Khalil, are you in some trouble?" My mother questioned.

"Why do you ask that, Ma? I just wanted to visit you." I said.

"No, I know something is up because it's past 10pm and you're at my house, with a fresh scratch above your eye and not to mention your wife" my mother tilted her head, "called here looking for you and she sounded distraught."

Sighing heavily, I began, "Ma, she cheated on me. I'm questioning if Rue is my baby and the dude had the nerve to have me arrested weeks ago!" I shouted in frustration.

"Okay, she cheated. Do you know that for sure, Khalil? I know my son and I know you're no angel. Y'all both did your dirt, but to put your hands on her, is something different! I didn't raise you to be hitting on women, now did I?" My mother got up and pointed in my face. "You are welcome to stay here as long as you need to, but you will not question my grand baby anymore!" Walking towards the kitchen, she turned to me to make sure it was clear. "Do you hear me, Khalil Taylor?"

I nodded my head. "Yeah Ma, but-"

"I said that's enough! Pilar is not just your girl or baby'd mother, that's your wife so you work that shit out!"

"I know mom, but I just can't right now. Pilar hurt me and before I hurt her, I need space." I pulled out a bottle of Henny from the cabinet.

"For once, you're hurt. How about those nights she called me because you were missing in action and I knew you were running the streets? Think about it, Khalil. I'm going to bed, goodnight!" She smiled and disappeared.

I know my mother was right, but my pride and ego was bruised. I wasn't going to be a sucker and take Pilar back, just that fast. Pilar was going to suffer, she knew she hurt me but I wanted her to see just how deep she cut me.

"I'm getting a DNA test, it's only right." I thought to myself, but if Pilar knew she probably wouldn't talk to me anymore, so I had to tread lightly when doing this.

Pilar

It was an understatement to say that Khalil wasn't feeling me, but honestly, I wanted my husband home. My life was draining and spiraling out of control, by the minute. Although I had my career, my kids, my car and house it just wasn't enough. Avery brought up a DNA test, I knew Khalil was Rue's father because she looked just like him, but my husband wasn't trying to hear that.

"I'ma just have to get her tested to prove that he is indeed, her father." I convinced myself. "I can't believe this is what my life has come to. I'm a statistic!"

Pulling out my journal, I decided I would write. I have been drinking non-stop and my problems are still here, so it is time to put the bottle down and figure this shit out.

Ring! Ring!
I reached over on the nightstand, in search of my phone. "Hello?"

"Hey baby, what time should I meet you?" My mother spoke into the phone.

Covering my mouth, I looked at the time. "Damn, in a half hour momma." I responded, jumping up in search of clothing.

"Don't tell me you were still sleeping, Pilar?"

"So, I won't tell you, but I already have Rue's clothes picked out." The phone went silent. "Momma I'm coming!" I shrieked.

"Hurry up, your appointment is at 8 am and I really don't want to put my grand baby through this anyway!" Carol added.

"I know, Ma." I hung-up the phone and rushed to get dressed.

Today was judgement day. I argued back and forth with the idea of getting the test done, but honestly, I wanted it to be set in stone that Khalil was her dad. It had been a week since I last saw him and when I called him I wanted it to be with good news.

Ring! Ring!
As I strapped Rue into her car seat, my phone rang. I figured it was my mom, so I paid it no mind, until it began to ring again.

Looking at the caller ID, it read: Que. I wasn't in the mood for him so I ignored the call.

Que flashed across my screen with a text message, which I ignored as well and headed to our appointment.

Two hours later and the test was completed. I was anxious for the results so I put a rush on it. I was happy I didn't run into Avery there, at the office. My father had called and said Khalil was on his way to the house to get Liam. I wanted to run into him and tell him about the test. My mother had left a half hour earlier than me so she could go get Liam dressed and ready.

Ring! Ring!

"Fuck, why is my phone ringing crazy?" Checking the ID, I saw that it was Jewel. I decided to call her back as soon as I reached my mother's house, my damn phone was on 3 percent. Placing my phone on the charger and dropping it in the seat, I pulled off. Driving and listening to music, I checked my mirror and saw Rue smiling up at me.

"Hey, baby! You up now?" I cooed. Hearing Rue coo back at me melted me. "I know, right, you wanna see daddy?" She opened her mouth and showed gums at the mention of Khalil.

"God please let this be his baby. I don't know how I can face him if the results turned-out otherwise." I pulled-over and picked-up my phone to send Khalil a text.

Pilar- hey Kha I know you can't stand me right now but I'm telling you I've never cheated on you, nor have I planned on this happening the way it has, I love you and I know I fucked up. I wanted to hurt you as much as you hurt me but then I became pregnant with Rue and nothing went as planned. You probably won't respond but I just had to let that out. Oh and FYI I've only slept with Avery once, if that makes a difference... One

Contemplating on whether to hit 'send', or not, I said to myself, "Fuck it, what do I have to lose." I hit the button and placed my phone back in the seat. Looking up at Rue, one more time, I jumped back on the highway, passing the Hilton hotel.

A car seemed to jump out of nowhere onto the road and tail behind me. I dismissed any ill feelings when I heard my phone bling that I had an incoming text. Speeding up, to lose the driver in the black Denali, I glanced down at my phone and saw it flash 'husband', causing me to smile.

Once again, I pulled-over and unhooked my seatbelt, to get a hold of my phone that had fallen. Picking it up, I looked back at Rue who was into her lullaby playing from the radio. I placed the phone in-between my thighs and hooked my seatbelt back.

Crash!

I felt my body jerk and my head hit the window. Dazed and in shock, I heard Rue's cries from the back seat. I struggled to lift my head up. I heard my door swing open and I was pulled from the car.

Falling to the ground, I tried to gain my bearings, as Rue's cries became faint. Grabbing at anything that would help me to get off of the ground, someone kicked me in the stomach, causing me to fall and roll over. Another kick came to the side of my face and everything started to fade, all while I stretched my arm out, in search of my baby.

Opening my eyes, I saw a guy carrying Rue as he hopped into the black Denali that was tailing me earlier.

"My- my- my baby!" I cried out and everything went completely black...

Khalil

"What the fuck?" I shouted in the bathroom. I had received a message from Pilar and I had replied over a half hour ago and she still had not responded.

"Khalil, is everything ok?" Carol asked knocking on the door.

"Nah." I said, unlocking the door. "Can you call Pilar from your line? She sent me a message and I replied, but she hasn't responded."

"Calm down, she was driving. I know she better not be texting and driving." Carol chastised.

"Yeah, you're right." Easing up a bit I went to sit in the living room and play with Liam.

"Daddy, what time is mommy coming? I thought we was going out as a family? You said that, right?" Liam asked, anxiously.

"Yes, Lil L., we're going out. She's on her way."

"Oh, my God!" Carol yelled from the kitchen.

Jumping up, I ran to her. "Ma, what's up?" I looked at the panicked look on her face and my stomach flipped. Covering her mouth, the tears just fell from her eyes as she pointed at the T.V.

"Pi- Pilar, that's Pilar's car on the news." She pointed at the T.V. I grabbed the remote and turned up the volume. Listening to the story, there was a hit and run on the Major Deegan and Pilar's car was a wreck. They had found her beside the car, unconscious and alone. Blinking my eyes, I stared at the T.V., bewildered.

"Alone? Alone?! I thought my baby was with her?!" I shouted.

"What happened?" Roger walked into the kitchen, hearing Carol and me yelling and shouting.

"Pilar was in an accident and they're saying she's alone! So where the fuck is my daughter?" I questioned, grabbing my phone off the counter.

"Where are you going?" Roger asked.

"I'm going to the hospital to see my wife and find-out where my daughter is!" I rushed out of the door leaving it half open.

Ring! Ring!

My phone buzzed as I raced to the hospital in search of answers.

"Hello?!"

"Khalil, I wanted to know if you had heard from Pilar? I-"

"Pilar is in the hospital and Rue is missing, Jewel! I don't know what happened but I'm going there now and I need to know where Rue is!" I shouted turning into the hospital's emergency room entrance.

"What do you mean? She had her with her. They were taking the DNA test." Jewel sobbed into the phone.

"The DNA test? Since when did she decide to do that?" I questioned.

"She made the appointment and went today, to prove to you that you're Rue's father."

"That's my fucking daughter. I don't care what no test says. I was there and that's my baby!" I shouted.

"Sir, Can I help you?" A receptionist asked as I removed the phone from my ear.

"Yes, I'm looking for my wife, Pilar Taylor. She was brought here from a car accident."

"Okay." The receptionist responded.

Placing the phone back to my ear, I spoke to Jewel. "I gotta go."

"Okay, I'm coming."

Hanging up, I looked at the receptionist, as she informed me: "Sir she's in ICU. That's on the 2nd floor."

I nodded my head to her. "Thanks." Running towards the elevator, to the second floor, I panicked.

"My wife is here, Pilar Taylor!" I shouted to the security guard.

"Okay, sir, calm down. We are going to get you to her."

Waiting up against the wall, I had all sorts of thoughts running through my mind. "What if she doesn't make it? Damn, I been acting shady to her and the day I decided I was gon' make amends, she's in ICU!" I paced back and forth, becoming impatient. "Fuck!" I hit the wall.

"Mr. Taylor, Mr. Taylor!" The Doctor called to me.

Stopping in my tracks, I responded. "Yes?"

"Your wife is in critical condition but she's stable. Her injuries are not life threatening, but she is sedated right now."

"So, can I see her?" I asked anxiously.

"Yes, right this way." The Doctor directed me.

"Khalil! Khalil!" Carol yelled out to me.

Stopping, so that she could catch-up to us, I explained. "Yeah, Ma, I'm heading to see Pilar now."

She fell-in step, next to me. Once we reached the room, I looked at Pilar and knew that my wife was in pain. Carol couldn't control her emotions. She started sobbing and walked out of the room.

Walking up to the side of the bed, I leaned in and whispered to Pilar. "Baby, I need you to pull through this." Moving her hair from her face, I spoke gently. "Pilar, I love you so much! I don't care what happened before today, I just need you to come home to us. We need you." The tears welled up in my eyes. I kissed her bruised cheek and left the room. Turning back, to look at her, once more, I mouthed: "I promise, I'm going to get whoever did this."

IT'S WAR...

The doctor gave me Pilar's belongings and I vanished. I wanted someone dead for this. Seeing Pilar laid-up and helpless had me dazed and enraged.

Ring! Ring! Pilar's phone was ringing.
"Hello?"

"Hello, who is this? Where's Pilar?"

"Andre, this is Khalil. Pilar is in the hospital." I spat.

"Hospital, for what? What happened? What the fuck is going on, Khalil? I've been calling her all morning. I know she did that DNA test with Avery, this morning, but- " Andre informed me, before I interrupted him.

"With Avery? She was with that nigga? Fuck that, somebody has my baby and now I think I know who it is!" I boasted into the phone.

"Yo, don't do nothing stupid, Khalil, wait for me!"

"Wait for you? Nah, I'm out! I gotta find this nigga!" I said, exiting the hospital.

"Yo, Kha, meet me on 3rd Avenue and 143rd. Come get me and we can figure this shit out!" Andre yelled. "Listen, your baby's life is at stake!"

Sighing, I hopped in the car and conceded. "Aight man, be ready. I'm gon' scoop up my people and then we can head over to that hotel."

I was pissed and anxious as I waited for Andre. Tony, Robert and Don showed up before him.

"Yo, waddup?" Robert said.

I filled them in on what had happened and the fact that my baby was missing. Andre pulled-up, shortly after.

I looked down at Pilar's phone at the text message that came through.

Que- Yo Ma I know you not fucking with me right now but watch out that bitch Chyanne is in town and she hyping up that when she see you it's on

Tossing the phone in the glove compartment, I wondered, out-loud: "Why the fuck is Que texting my wife and where the fuck is Chyanne?"

"Chyanne! Chyanne fuck with Avery! I thought I told you!" Andre said from the window.

"Nah, nigga, you didn't tell me that shit! You know what, fuck it! Why would you tell, when you want my wife as well!" I accused, starting up the car.

"Khalil, it's not even like that, but later for that, we gotta go see where this dude is and get your daughter safe, then we can handle him and then Chyanne!" Andre reasoned.

"Whatever, yo!" As we drove to the hotel, where Avery was staying, Pilar's phone started to ring.

Ring! Ring!

"Dre, answer that!" I said

"Yo, who this?" Dre spoke into the phone.

"Don't demand shit, I ask the questions! Where that nigga Khalil at?" The caller asked.

"He's driving. Talk to me!" He put the phone on speaker.

"Tell him he will get his daughter if the DNA test proves he's the father"

"Nigga I am her fucking father, fuck you mean?" Khalil yelled.

He laughed. "Oh, that's what your wife wants you to think, is that before or after she fucked me and left your ass for her baby father?"

Screwing up his face, Khalil shouted, "Fuck your bitch ass! Trust, your day is coming, muthafucka!"

Robert tapped his shoulder. "Relax man. He wanna get you tight."

"You gon' get your DNA test and when the test proves I'm the father you're going to look stupid! Pussy ass nigga, chasing a female who doesn't want you!" Khalil laughed. "Pathetic ass nigga!"

"I'll call you in 3 days, when the results are back, playa." Avery spoke, teasing Khalil and with that the call was dropped.

Khalil clinched his fists as he hopped out of the car, on the side of the road, screaming and shouting to himself.

"Yo, Kha, get back in the car man!" Tony shouted.

"Nah, I got him." Robert stopped Tony before he exited the car.

"Aight, cool." Tony relaxed.

"Yo Rob, let Khalil know I know where his kid and BM stay at, if he tryna go that route!" Andre spoke.

"Copy." Robert exited and walked up on Khalil. "Yo, Dre said he know where his baby mama and kid stay if you wanna get at him!"

"Nah, I'm not into snatching kids, but where his BM work because they fucked-up my wife. I'ma pay her ass a visit." Khalil said through clenched teeth.

"A'ight we could send Don and Tony wild asses out there." Robert suggested.

"Nah, send Dre before I kill him. He been fucking my wife."

"Nigga I know my sister did some wild shit, this past year, but what I do know is, she isn't fucking Andre, not after the way he played her. We are closer than we appear to be Kha, trust me." Robert said, pulling Khalil in. "He could be of good use, here. Besides, he wanna get at Avery for what happened at the club that night."

"Yeah, you right. Aight let's set this up, then I'm headed back to the hospital to be with my wife." Khalil walked back to the car.

"Yo, we got a plan, but we gon' head to my crib to map it out." Robert said to the group.

In Rob's crib...

"So, wassup?" Tony asked, ready to get to work.

"Have a drink, calm down, cuz these next few days are not gonna be fun and games." Khalil said.

"Copy." The fellas said in unison.

Pulling out a bottle of Henny and getting seated in the living room, Khalil spoke to the group. "So, word is, Dre knows where Avery baby mother and son stay at, but like I told Rob I'm not into snatching kids up, but his baby mama, Ima holla at her."

Pointing at Don and Tony, "That's where y'all come into play. I want you to show up at her job and snatch her up. Don't hit her! I repeat, don't hit shorty unless it calls for it, aight?" Khalil stared at Tony. "I'm looking at you cuz you the wild one. I want y'all to antagonize her until she gives us all the info we need on Avery." Khalil took a gulp of the Hennessy.

"Aight and then what happens?" Don asked.

"That's when I need you to pay a visit to his crib, send a warning, and let him know we not playing fair and we know where he stay at."

"What's that supposed to do Kha?" Tony asked.

"Just follow the rules. We can't get too crazy because he has my daughter." Khalil sighed, shaking his head.

"Andre, I want you to head to Chyanne crib. Now that we know she's been fucking with Avery, she knows something. I'm putting you on her because y'all share a kid and I need him outta harm's way." Khalil said, looking off.

"Me and Rob gon' head to the hotel and use Rob girl to get in the room."

"Rob girl? Who the fuck is that? Do Rue even know her?" Tony jumped up. "Kha that's my god daughter and I swear-" Khalil raised his hand to stop Tony's rant.

"So, who do you suggest then, Tony?" Khalil shouted.

"Tell Jewel, she's her godmother and she's a thorough chick!" Tony suggested.

"Let me call her, then. Hold that thought." With that, Khalil pulled out his phone.

"Yo, Ma you still at the hospital?"

"Yeah, Khalil, why wassup?" Jewel asked apprehensively.

"I need you to do us a solid and get into the hotel room where Avery is staying and get my baby girl." Khalil sighed. "Jewel I'm trust-"

Jewel cut him off. "Say no more. I'll get my baby out of there safe. Now, if I find out Chyanne grimey-ass had something to do with it, I get to handle her, Khalil."

"You got it. Listen out for my call or matter of fact, meet us at Rob's crib."

"Aight, be there in 15 minutes." She ended the call.

"She's in." Khalil said. "So, that's the plan. Let's book y'all tickets now."

Four hours later, Andre, Khalil, Robert and Jewel sat around waiting for Tony's call that they had touched down at Sariya's job. Sariya was scheduled to get off work at 11pm, so they had an hour to kill and scope out the area.

"Yo, when are they going to reach that bitch house?" Jewel jumped up, anxious to hear some word on their progress. "I'm ready to get my niece and find Chyanne!"

"Relax, shorty!" Khalil chuckled "We gon let you get your fair share of beating her."

"I'm going to kill her Khalil! I'm going to kill her!" Jewel boasted.

"But not until after I get my baby." Khalil mentioned.

Andre twisted up his nose at jewel. "Just calm down, Jewel. We need you level headed."

Jewel turned her attention to Andre. "Oh, you getting soft because that's your baby mother?"

"Never that, she deserves everything coming to her, if she's down with that shit. Trust me, I'm on your team!" Andre said.

"You better be!" Jewel warned.

The waiting game...
Ring! Ring!
"Yo!" Khalil answered.

"Yeah, we got shorty. She don't give two shits about Avery and she's ready to give him up!"

"Copy, get everything from her." Khalil stated calmly.

"No doubt!" Don hung up.

They all headed to the hotel, to sit outside.

Meanwhile, in the hotel room, Rue was crying, nonstop.

"Hello, shut her up! What the fuck?" Chyanne shouted.

"You shut the fuck up, stupid. Don't be telling me about my child! You lost your rabbit ass mind?" Avery shouted across the room.

"You don't even know if this is your kid stupid! It could very well be her husbands!"

Chyanne twisted up her lip. "Sprung on this bitch! Typical." She mumbled under her breath.

"Yeah, aight, say something else stupid and I'm going to knock you out, Chyanne!" Avery shouted.

"Whatever. I'm stepping-out. Put her to sleep, Avery." Chyanne waved her hand and walked out.

Pulling up to the hotel, Andre spotted Chyanne. "Yo, she's right there! Chyanne is right there!" Looking-on, Jewel jumped up.

"Relax, she gotta go back into the room soon. Let's parlay for a while."

"We better hurry up!" Jewel shouted.

"Call Tony and tell him to send the picture to Avery phone, of Sariya tied up!" Khalil shouted.

Robert called Tony. "Yo, send that pic to Avery, we got Chyanne."

"Copy, copy." He hung-up. We watched and waited on Chyanne's next move.

Jewel got out of the car and waited in the staircase upstairs, for Chyanne.

Beeping through to Jewel, Khalil whispered, "Listen out good, aight?"

Andre waited outside the hotel to catch up with Chyanne. Chyanne came running with the phone to her ear, stopping short at Andre.

I could see the exchange between them but I couldn't hear what they were saying.

Andre walked-off putting up his hand, to signal we were good. Once she was in the elevator, I placed a call to Jewel, that she was all good.

Once upstairs, Chyanne flew off the elevator and straight to the room, just as Jewel was coming out of the staircase. Putting a gun to the back of her head, Jewel hissed, "If you scream, I will kill you, right now!" Chyanne shook her head in fear.

"What I want you to do is hand me my god daughter with no drama, or we will have Andrew hurt in the process of killing you!"

Chyanne nodded again. "You can have her." Rolling her eyes, she pulled out her key to the room, unlocking the door.

"Hurry your ass up!" Avery shouted from the bathroom.

Chyanne went to the bedroom and picked up Rue. Grabbing her blanket, she walked out to the front.

"What the fuck are you doing? I just put her to sleep." Avery shouted, as she passed him, with the baby in her arms.

"Listen, Avery I can't do this shit. You don't love me and I have a son of my own to worry about!" She said, reaching for the door. "You can fight your own battles alone that come with taking this kid."

Opening the door, she handed Rue to Jewel. Jewel walked down the stairs with the sleeping baby. Jewel exited the building, toting Rue to the car. Jumping out of the car, Khalil grabbed Rue, kissing and hugging her.

"Jewel, take her to Carol. We gon' set up the warehouse. See you there." Khalil grinned.

Jewel grabbed Rue back and Andre placed a call to Tony letting him know that we were all clear.

"Aight, let's go!" Khalil said as Jewel hopped into a taxi.

Avery exited the hotel with a duffle bag in hand, yelling at Chyanne.

"Stupid bitch, you gave my child up! I should kill you!"

"That's not your baby! She doesn't even look like you, asshole!" Chyanne snapped back, entering the parking lot behind him.

Avery turned and punched her in the face. Chyanne fell to the floor, grabbing her face "You put your hands on me! Are you crazy?!"

Just as he bent down to Chyanne's level, Khalil kicked him in the back, causing him to fall over. Throwing a pillow case over his face, he held the gun to Avery's temple.

"Let's roll!" Khalil commanded.

Andre grabbed Chyanne off the ground. "I don't have time to play games with you today, Chyanne, just come with me!"

Throwing them into the back of the Range Rover, they headed to the warehouse.

"When I find out who set me up, y'all are dead!" Avery shouted.

"Nigga, shut up! Your ass is dead before you even find out!" Robert swung back and hit him over the head twice, with the butt of the gun, causing him to lose consciousness.

"Oh, my God!" Chyanne covered her mouth. "Look, I wasn't in on this plan. I just wanted to hurt Pilar, not take the baby!"

Khalil lost his cool and smacked her. "You stupid bitch! You wanted to hurt her? You nearly killed her!" Khalil raised his hand again, but Andre stopped him.

"Listen, let's not ruin it for her."

"Ruin what for me?" Chyanne asked in shock.

They pulled up to the warehouse. They all exited the vehicle...

Pilar

Coming to my senses, I looked around the room. As I tried to get up, my entire body ached.

"Help, help me!" I whispered, trying to scream, but my voice cracked. Reaching for the button, I pressed on it. My mother and the nurse came running in.

"Are you okay? How do you feel?" The nurse asked, concerned.

I jumped up, panicking, almost forgetting the pain! Although my neck hurt and I couldn't speak too loudly, I managed to get it out. "I'm, I'm okay."
My eyes searched the room. "Where's Rue? My baby, they took her."

My mother rushed to my side. "Calm down, baby, calm down." She said, rubbing my arm, trying to soothe me "They are out looking for her."

The tears welled up in my eyes, just as my mother's phone began to ring.

"Hello?"

"Hey, Ma, tell Pilar we have Rue. She's here with Tamia and Tasha." Jewel said.

"Oh, okay. Thank you, baby!" Carol hung up. "Rue is with Tamia and Tasha. They have her safe and you can relax."

Laying back on the bed, I sighed. "Khalil? Where is he?"

"He's fine. He's out handling business." Carol said pulling up a chair.

"Okay. I need someone to check my mailbox tomorrow for the results, so I can put an end to our feud." Closing my eyes, I drifted back off to sleep...

The final Chapter

Jewel, Tony and Don joined us in the warehouse.

"Take off the cases." Khalil said

Once our faces were exposed and the dim light shined on everyone's faces, Avery looked on in shock. "You bitch ass niggas! I can't believe y'all!" He struggled to break free from the ropes.

"You might as well relax, cuz you can't get free, playa! You had my kid taken away and my wife beaten!" I tapped the gun on Avery's face. "Tssk, you messed up, bruh!"

"What? I never had Pilar beat up that was this chick being envious and letting her emotions get the best of her!" Avery shouted.

"Oh, so it was your idea to beat my wife? Just when I thought I was going to let you off, I hear this." I pointed the gun at Chyanne. "Which one should I shoot first?" I alternated pointing the gun between the two.

"Let her free! Let her free, Khalil!" Jewel shouted.

I looked over and saw the vengeance in Jewels face. I ordered Robert to untie her and Jewel pounced on her until Chyanne was screaming.

"That's enough, Jewel." Pulling her off of Chyanne was a task.

"You nearly killed my sister, my best friend!" Jewel shouted. Finally calming down, Jewel huffed and puffed, leaning up against the wall.

Shaking his head, Avery watched in nervous amusement. "Oh, so what which one of y'all niggas wanna fight me? Trust me, it's not gon' be that easy!" He boasted.

Feeling my phone vibrate, I took it from my pocket. It flashed 'Carol'. I ignored the call. The phone vibrated, again.

"You gon get that, nigga?" Avery chuckled.

Pulling the trigger on the gun, I hit him right in the middle of his forehead.

"I had enough of his ass! Do what y'all want with her. Andre, you can get rid of his body, however you see fit, since I didn't give you a chance to get a piece of him." Walking out of the warehouse, turned around and looked back at them. "Thanks y'all. I'm going to see about my wife"...

2 months later... Pilar

That following day, we had received the results and Khalil is Rue's father.

Chyanne's body was found by the Hudson River with a single gunshot to the heart and lastly Avery's body still has yet to be found.

Here it is 2 months later and I'm healed and ready to celebrate my 30th birthday with my family and friends. Khalil has planned a lavish all white yacht party. I was elated.

Looking myself over in the mirror, smoothing out my Vera Wang gown, I exited the room and headed to the boat dock.

"Before we sail the ocean I want to propose a toast!" I said, smiling. "I have so much to celebrate!"

"Well, I hope this celebration doesn't involve your concoction of 1 Glass of Wine and 2 Shots of Patron!"
The dock erupted in laughter...

And that's how dating landed me in this whirlwind of drama...

Muah!!! —Pilar

About the author

Theresa "Reese" Kirk represents new self - published authors. Hailing from the boogie down Bronx, New York she has started her writing expedition in 2015. With her love for reading and writing in just a year she has self - published 3 books, 2 of which is poetry and 1 novel. Theresa has a day job and uses all her free time to write anything that comes to her mind. Always using writing as an outlet to overcome her being antisocial, but she finally started putting her ideas out for the world to see. Shy yet outgoing Theresa is far from finish when it comes to writing, it has become so natural in her life, so keep watch out for all her upcoming books.

Made in the USA
Middletown, DE
16 September 2016